MONTANA MAVERICKS

Welcome to Big Sky Country, home of the Montana Mavericks! Where free-spirited men and women discover love on the range.

THE TRAIL TO TENACITY

Tenacity is the town that time forgot, home of down-to-earth cowboys who'd give you the (denim) shirt off their back. Through the toughest times, they've held their heads high, and they've never lost hope. Take a ride out this way and get to know the neighbors—you might even meet the maverick of your dreams!

Chrissy Hastings thought she'd never get over Hayes Parker, her high school sweetheart. Eventually, though, she grew up. She got married to someone else; she had a life. Though her marriage failed, she still believes in love. If she's honest, she still believes in Hayes, even after all these years...

Dear Reader,

Can you believe it? This year, the beloved Montana Mavericks series is celebrating thirty years of engaging, emotional Western love stories. And to mark this exciting milestone, we are introducing a whole new Montana Mavericks hometown.

Tenacity, Montana, lives up to its name. It's a hardscrabble ranching town smack-dab in the heart of Big Sky Country. You have to work hard to make it in Tenacity.

Hayes Parker grew up there. But he left right after high school, vowing never to return. For years, he's kept that vow. But trouble at home draws him back. And right away he runs into the girl who broke his heart all those years ago.

In the decade and a half since Chrissy Hastings had to walk away from Hayes, she's left town, too—and loved and lost a second time. Now she's returned to Tenacity to start over. Neither Chrissy nor Hayes has any intention of fanning the embers of their long-ago love.

However, when she needs a helping hand, Hayes reaches out. They agree to keep it strictly friends only. But their yearning hearts have other plans.

I hope this story grabs you and won't let you go till the very last page. And thank you for making the Montana Mavericks series a reader favorite for three decades and counting.

Happy reading everyone,

Christine Rimmer

REDEEMING THE MAVERICK

CHRISTINE RIMMER

H Harlequin

MONTANA MAVERICKS

Special thanks and acknowledgment are given to Christine Rimmer for her contribution to the Montana Mavericks: The Trail to Tenacity miniseries.

 Harlequin®

MONTANA MAVERICKS

Recycling programs for this product may not exist in your area.

ISBN-13: 978-1-335-14312-9

Redeeming the Maverick

Copyright © 2024 by Harlequin Enterprises ULC

Harlequin Enterprises ULC
22 Adelaide St. West, 41st Floor
Toronto, Ontario M5H 4E3, Canada
www.Harlequin.com

Printed in Lithuania

MIX
Paper | Supporting responsible forestry
FSC® C021394

Christine Rimmer came to her profession the long way around. She tried everything from acting to teaching to telephone sales. Now she's finally found work that suits her perfectly. She insists she never had a problem keeping a job—she was merely gaining "life experience" for her future as a novelist. Christine lives with her family in Oregon. Visit her at christinerimmer.com.

Visit the Author Profile page
at Harlequin.com for more titles.

This book is dedicated to Susan Litman, our fabulous lead editor for this long-running, much-loved Montana Mavericks series. Thank you, Susan, for so smartly and conscientiously guiding each Montana Mavericks story all the way from conception to publication—and somehow always managing to tackle every challenge with skill, patience and heart.

Chapter One

They say you can't go home again, and that was just fine with Hayes Parker. He'd left the End of the Road Ranch on the day he graduated from Tenacity High School vowing never to return. For fifteen years, Hayes had kept that vow.

But hey. Never say never.

In early June of his thirty-third year, Hayes's older brother Braden called.

"The ranch is in big trouble," Braden said flatly. "As for Dad, he's worse than ever, barking orders right and left. Nowadays, the man is incapable of a civil conversation. He's just plain unbearable to be around."

Hayes was thinking that none of that was news, but he took the high road and kept the snarky comment to himself.

Braden wasn't finished. "Miles is off in the service and unreachable." Miles was the youngest of the three brothers. "As for Rylee, she's engaged, and living in Bronco."

Hayes felt the sharp pinch of regret. Rylee was the youngest of the four of them, their only sister. And Hayes had never kept in touch the way he knew he should. He drew a slow breath. "Rylee's engaged..."

"Yeah. To Shep Dalton."

"Wow." Rylee and Shep had been friends in school—

just friends, the way Hayes remembered it. "The years do go by…"

Braden said, "She's got herself a big-time job in Bronco." A hundred miles from their hardscrabble hometown of Tenacity, Montana, Bronco was bigger, greener—and for some families, richer. "I'm telling you, Hayes, no way Rylee has time to deal with Dad, let alone to take on the near-impossible task of saving the ranch."

"I hear you," Hayes replied. Because he did and he sympathized. But that didn't mean he'd be headed for Tenacity imagining he could save the day.

"I'm done," Braden said darkly. "Finished. On my way out the door. I've stuck it out as long as I can stand to. But no more. I'm leaving."

Hayes tried to find the right words. Too bad there were none.

"Hayes? You still there?"

"I'm here. And, Braden, I get it. And I wish you well. But I'm not going home to try to deal with Dad. I gave all that up when I was eighteen. You have to know that."

There was a silence, a silence weighted with grim understanding on both their parts.

Braden asked in a hollow voice, "Not even to save the family ranch?"

Hayes felt a tug deep down inside him. He hated that ranch. But he loved it, too. Even after fifteen years, it was all tangled up for him, the hurt. The frustration. The clear knowledge that he needed to get out or there would be no hope for him. "Uh-uh," he said quietly into the phone. "I'm not coming back. No can do."

Braden let out a heavy sigh. "I understand."

"Sorry, brother."

"Hey. It was worth a shot. You take care now."

"Let me know where you end up," Hayes said.

"Will do." Braden said goodbye.

Hayes hung up the phone determined to stand his ground. Yeah, the very idea that the ranch might fall out of Parker family hands…it got to him, it hit him deep. True, he'd vowed never to go back there. But that didn't change the way he felt about the ranch. It was Parker land. And it damn well ought to remain that way whether Hayes ever set foot there again or not.

He told himself to let it go, that he wasn't going back and there was no upside to stewing about it.

But over the next couple of months, thoughts of home nagged at him. There had been good things back home. He'd found first love there, deep and true. At least for as long as it had lasted.

Since then, he'd been married—and widowed. He'd loved his wife with all his heart. And yet sometimes he still thought of Chrissy Hastings, his high school sweetheart. Of her long brown hair and big brown eyes, her sweet laugh and kind heart. It had cut him deep, losing Chrissy. But still, he'd moved on.

In the past fifteen years, he'd worked on ranches all over the Western states. Now, he was top hand on a fine spread called the Bar-M up in northern Montana near the town of Rust Creek Falls. The owner's son on the Bar-M was ready to step up as top hand, so Hayes knew he'd be leaving here soon anyway—and when he did, he would finally buy his own land and build his own spread. He refused to go backward. Why in hell should he help out the father who'd rarely given him anything but grief?

But then, on the last day of July, his mother called.

He considered not answering. Over the years, he'd let most of his mom's calls go to voicemail. She was such a good mom. He still missed her every day—and talking to her just made him long for the home he'd left behind.

She was the easy one to love, always gentle, thoughtful and full of understanding. The truth was, he'd always hated hearing the pain in her voice. It hurt so bad when she said how much she missed him.

He'd missed her a lot, too. But overall, it just worked better not to poke at a deep wound.

This time, though, he couldn't stop himself from taking the damn call. "Hi, Mom."

Norma sighed. "Hayes. It's so good to hear your voice."

He had to swallow to loosen the sudden tightness in his throat. "How are you?"

"I'm okay, honey. Doing well…" The words trailed off into silence. Finally, she spoke again. "I'm just going to go ahead and put it out there."

He rubbed at the space between his eyebrows where tension had gathered. "Mom, look—"

"Please, honey. Hear me out."

He should say he had to go and then hang up quick.

But he did no such thing. "What, Mom?"

"Your father, well, he's sick. And he's been sick for a while now."

Sick? Not possible. Lionel Parker was too ornery to get sick. "Sick with what, Mom?"

"We're not sure. For months, he's been having horrible bellyaches with fever, and his stomach bloating up. Up till now, he's always gotten better for a while, at least—but then he ends up in bed, sick and in pain with a fever all over again."

"What does the doctor say?"

"Hayes." Her soft voice held the patience of the ages. "I can't get him to go to the doctor…"

Hayes rubbed that spot between his eyes a little harder.

Of course, Lionel Parker refused to find out what was wrong with him. Lionel Parker didn't get sick. Getting sick would prove he was only human like everyone else.

His mom continued, "He says he'll be fine, that we can't afford to 'throw money away' on doctors. And honey, the hard fact is we're dead broke." She hesitated. And then she laid it on him. "We haven't lost the ranch yet, but it could happen if things don't turn around." Her words only confirmed what Braden had said two months ago. As though she sensed the direction of his thoughts, she added, "Braden picked up stakes and left."

"I know, Mom. He called me before he took off. Tell me you at least hired someone to help out."

She didn't answer. Her silence felt weighted with reproach.

"Right," he muttered. "You already said there's no money."

"Rylee has offered to take a leave from the great job she loves. She's director of marketing now for the Bronco Convention Center." His mother's voice was full of pride. But then she added wearily, "Hayes, it's just wrong to ask her to give up the job she's worked so hard to earn."

"I get it, Mom. I do."

"Did you know she's going to marry—"

"Shep Dalton. Yeah. Braden told me. I'm glad for her."

"Oh, Hayes…"

At his feet, his dog, Rayna, made a low, anxious sound. He shifted his gaze down to her. She'd sensed his mood. Now she stared up at him through worried eyes. He gave her a quick scratch on her furry head.

And his mom finally hit him with the big question. "Do you think you might possibly see your way clear to come on home for a bit?" Hayes could hear the tears in her voice. She was trying so hard not to cry.

Those unshed tears broke him.

He found himself thinking that he really needed to get over himself. He was no longer an overgrown boy with a heart full of grievances. Uh-uh. Now he was a grown-ass man who'd loved and lost—twice.

It was about time he tried to put the past behind him. "Okay, Mom. I'll be there tomorrow."

She burst into tears then.

He soothed her as best he could, offering reassurances that everything was going to be all right while at the same time wondering if he'd somehow lost his mind.

When he hung up with her, he texted Braden to let him know what was going on.

And the next morning, as dawn painted the purple sky with streaks of orange, Hayes packed up his crew cab, hitched up his horse trailer and clicked his tongue for his dog. Rayna jumped right up onto the passenger seat. She was a big girl, a hundred-pound Bulgarian shepherd, long-haired and bred to live on the land guarding and protecting livestock. His late wife, Anna, had raised her from a pup, treating her like one of the family. As a result, Rayna was more pet than guardian dog.

"You ready to go?" he asked.

Rayna gave a low whine in answer.

"All right. Let's hit the road."

It was a seven-hour drive to Tenacity—seven and a half counting a stop to let his horse stretch his legs. They rolled into Hayes's dusty hometown at 1:30 in the afternoon. He drove down Central Avenue thinking that things hadn't changed all that much.

The local watering hole, the Grizzly Bar, still had that

flat roof, like most of the commercial buildings in town. And it still had a big orange door with weather-beaten benches to either side and a rough façade of bricks made from natural stone. Directly across the street from the Grizzly was Tenacity's one bus stop complete with a bench, a sign and a plexiglass shelter where you could catch the Trailways bus that rolled by twice daily going southwest toward Bronco, or northeast to the North Dakota border.

And if he drove on a few more blocks, he'd be leaving town. In no time, he'd find himself rolling onto Hayes family land.

But he wasn't ready for that. Not yet.

Instead, he went left at the next intersection and then left again. That had him ending up not far from where he'd turned off the highway in the first place. Pulling into the parking lot of the Tenacity Inn, he stopped beneath the porte cochere next to the lobby doors.

The way he saw it, he needed someplace to escape to, just in case. A room for the night would do just fine. That way, if his dad really drove him up the wall, he'd have a place to hole up for a few hours—after he put his horse out to pasture, somehow managed to get his pigheaded father to visit the damn doctor and saw to the evening chores.

Did they allow pets as big as Rayna here?

One way to find out.

He let the dog out. She promptly peed on a big, rounded landscaping rock. Luckily it didn't look like she'd hit any of the decorative plantings. Hayes decided to call that a win. From the trailer his sorrel gelding, Roscoe, nickered softly.

"Won't be long now," he called to the horse. Roscoe snorted once and let it go at that.

Hayes ran up the steps and pulled open the glass door to the lobby, ushering Rayna in ahead of him. Inside, the Tenacity Inn was nothing fancy, but it was clean with a nice, big lobby and plenty of windows to let in the afternoon light.

He led Rayna straight to the front desk, where he swept off his hat and asked for a room. The pretty blonde desk clerk said that she could reserve him a room, but he couldn't check in until three—and yes, he could have his dog with him as long as the dog was quiet and well trained.

Rayna could bark with the best of them whenever she sensed a threat. She was bred to guard livestock, after all. But Hayes kept his mouth shut about that.

"Yeah," he said. "She's a good dog, easy-natured and well behaved. Sit, girl." Rayna tucked in her low, furry tail and dropped to her haunches. She was something. She sat there looking nothing short of regal, waiting for his next command.

The blonde nodded approvingly. "She's a calm one, I can see that," she said as she took Hayes's credit card.

The clerk had just handed him his room key when some-one behind him gasped—and somehow, right then, just from that one sharp, indrawn breath, he *knew*. "Hayes?" the woman behind him asked in complete disbelief. "Is that you?"

He'd been in town for a matter of minutes. And some-how, already, the past had caught up with him.

He made himself turn to face her.

Damn. She looked great. Beautiful as always, but not the same girl he used to know. She was all woman now.

Her face was a little thinner, her cheekbones more pro-nounced. Her seal-brown hair was pulled back and an-chored in a thick knot at the back of her head. Her eyes were exactly as he remembered them, deep brown around the iris, raying out to amber and green rimmed with gray. He saw sadness in those eyes—pride and grit, too.

"Chrissy," he said rough and low.

Those soft, full lips were slightly parted in surprise. "What are you doing here?" She asked the question quietly, her voice carefully controlled.

He took his time answering because he needed a moment to catch his breath. Even though she'd spoken to him in a soft and civil tone, to have her standing right here in front of him felt like a slap in the face.

It was bad enough he was about to go try to deal with his old man for the first time in a decade and a half. But Chrissy...

That was a punch to the gut all over again.

She glanced down at Rayna. "Who's this?"

"My dog. Her name's Rayna."

"Hey, Rayna," Chrissy said. Rayna tipped up her big head, awaiting strokes. Chrissy gave her what she wanted.

He explained, "My dad's sick and there's no one to help out. You could say I drew the short straw. What about you?"

"I'm the catering manager here at the inn."

"I heard you got married," he said, playing it casual for all he was worth.

She lifted one shoulder in a sad little shrug. "I'm divorced now."

He'd had no idea. "Sorry to hear that."

"Uh, thank you," she replied stiffly. *God, this is awful*, he thought. And then she asked, "You?"

He gave her the truth. "I was married. My wife died..."

Those big eyes got shiny. She looked like she might cry. "Oh, Hayes. I'm so sorry..."

Way to go, Parker, he thought. He'd developed a real knack lately for making women cry—yesterday, his mom. Today, his first love.

With a tiny sniff, Chrissy glanced away, out toward the

porte cochere and his truck and horse trailer waiting beneath it. He looked her over some more. Because he couldn't stop himself.

She had one of those word tattoos in a delicate font wrapped around her left forearm: *Be Bold. Be True. Be Free.*

That tattoo surprised him. The Chrissy he used to know wasn't the type to get inked. He wondered so many things—like why the tattoo and how she had ended up divorced.

His brothers had never said a word about her in all the years he'd been gone—probably because they knew the subject of Chrissy was a painful one for him. Now and then, though, he would check in with his buddies in town. From them, he'd learned that Chrissy had finished college with a degree in hospitality, that she'd married a successful accountant. The last he'd heard, she and her husband were doing great over in Wonderstone Ridge, a resort town down the road toward Bronco.

Was it the divorce that had her choosing to move back home?

Not that it was any of his business.

"Well," she said, drawing her shoulders back, her lips tipping up in a cool smile, "I should get to work…"

"Good to see you, Chrissy." It was only halfway a lie.

Her smile wavered just a little. "You too, Hayes. Take care."

"Thanks." He tipped his hat to her as he settled it back on his head. And then, clicking his tongue for his dog, he turned for the door. Chrissy made no effort to slow him down.

He went out into the bright August sunlight reminding himself that he was bound to run into her at some point and it was just as well he'd gotten that over with quick.

His pulse roared in his ears as he opened the passenger

door of his truck and clicked his tongue at his dog. Rayna jumped up to the seat.

And then, for a minute that seemed to stretch into eternity, he just stood there with the door open, staring blindly at his dog, his heart beating like a wrecking ball in the cage of his chest.

At the ranch, things were every bit as bad as he'd expected.

The iron sign above the main gate had come loose on one side. Both the barn and the house needed repainting. The tractor shed and the chicken coop cried out for a fresh coat of whitewash. A quick glance around showed him that shingles were missing from just about every roof. A rusted pickup with two flat tires sat in the dirt next to the rough rail fence that surrounded the house.

And other fences were clearly down. Chickens scattered, stirring up dust, as he drove in. By the rail fence, a black Angus cow nibbled at Norma Parker's wilted roses while a baldy calf stuck his nose under the bottom rail to crop at the fringe of grass on the other side.

Hayes pulled to a stop by the low gate that opened onto a natural stone walk leading up to the front porch steps. For a long string of seconds, he just sat there, engine idling, dreading getting out, not wanting to face what waited inside.

And then the front door opened. His mom, looking worn and weary beyond her years, stepped out. With a cry, she rushed down the steps.

That got him moving. He shut off the engine and jumped from the cab in time to catch her when she threw herself into his arms.

"Hayes! Oh, honey... I'm so glad you're here." She

stared up at him, dark circles beneath her eyes, tears on her cheeks. "Look at you. More handsome than ever..." A sob escaped her.

"Hey, Mom. Hey..." He pulled her in for one more hug before asking grimly, "How is he?"

She sniffled and swiped at her eyes with a work-roughened hand. "It's bad, honey. He won't listen to me. We have to do something."

He clasped her shoulders. "I need to take care of my horse. I'll be quick. And then I'll be in."

She squeezed his arm. "Hurry."

"I will."

Fifteen minutes later, he instructed Rayna to wait on the porch and went inside, where everything looked pretty much as he remembered—only older and more worn out.

"No damn doctor!" It was his father's voice, rough, angry and full of pain. The sound came from the master bedroom across the great room and down a short hallway.

His mother answered, "But you're ill, Lionel. You're sick enough that you're scaring me." She said something else, but Hayes couldn't make out the words.

"No, Norma," blustered his dad. "I'll be all right. Just leave me be!"

His mom started shouting then. "Lionel Parker, you are spiking a fever of a hundred and two! This cannot go on!"

His dad launched into more objections as Hayes started walking. His boots echoing on the worn wood floor, he strode toward the bedroom.

The door was open. He hesitated at the threshold, shocked at what he saw.

His dad lay on his back on the old iron-frame bed, his belly enormous, his face heavy, unshaven, his scruffy beard dead white, his skin yellowish and his eyes red-rimmed.

Those eyes locked right on him. "Well. If it isn't the prodigal son coming home at last…" Lionel Parker's insult died on his lips as he pressed his hands to his belly and moaned in pain.

Hayes swept off his hat. "Hey, Dad. Real good to see you, too. I'm here to help Mom get you to the hospital."

"No!" Lionel clutched his stomach even harder and groaned again. "We can't afford—"

"You're going, Dad."

"Do not call me any damn ambulance!"

"Okay, I won't." Hayes spoke to his mother. "Let's get him in my truck."

"I'm not going anywhere," growled Lionel.

"That's what you think, Dad."

Lionel kept saying no, but somehow Hayes managed to sit him up, put his slippers on him and drag him to his feet. From there, Hayes slung Lionel's beefy right arm across his shoulders. Norma pulled Lionel's left arm around her neck so she could support the old man on his other side.

They started walking. Lionel objected with each step. More than once, he almost got loose. But he was in bad shape and could barely stand on his own. Hayes kept a strong hold on his wrist and around his swollen middle as they went.

Somehow, they got him out the front door, where Rayna was waiting.

"Stay," Hayes commanded. Rayna sat.

With his dad sagging between them, Hayes and his mom staggered down the steps and across the walk. Norma ran around the truck bed and got in the crew cab's back seat on the far side. Hayes boosted Lionel up as Norma did the best she could to pull him into the cab.

"I'll stay back here with him," his mom said as she gently hooked up his seat belt for him.

Hayes glanced at his dog, who sat watching him from the porch. He hoped the rail fence would be enough to keep her close to the house. "Stay!" he shouted once more.

She gave him a worried-sounding whine.

Hayes shut the front gate, then ran around and got in behind the wheel. As he buckled himself in, his mom said, "I put in a little fountain in the backyard a few years ago. Your dog will have water when she needs it."

"Thanks, Mom. That's great." He started up the truck and headed for Bronco. Once they reached the highway, he kept the speed just over the limit while constantly fighting the urge to floor it and get them there quicker.

His mom called Bronco Valley Hospital from the back seat to let them know they were bringing Lionel in. As the miles rolled away beneath the crew cab's wheels, Lionel stared straight ahead, a grim scowl on his face. Hayes appreciated the quiet. But every time he glanced in the rearview mirror and met his mother's worried eyes, dread marched like cold fingers up and down his spine.

His father was in bad shape. Hayes was not a praying man as a rule. But he was praying now.

Chapter Two

A woman and a man, both in scrubs, were waiting with a gurney when Hayes stopped at the curb twenty feet from the doors to Emergency.

Norma went in with Lionel while Hayes parked his truck. He was worried sick for his father—yeah, he and his dad shared a boatload of animosity between them. All that anger and resentment wasn't likely to be resolved anytime soon.

But for Hayes, at least, the love was still there. His dad had been a good dad until Hayes reached his teens. Until then, Lionel was a strict father, but he moderated his toughness with patience and affection.

And then times got harder, money got tighter, and Lionel got worried. His worry translated itself into harsh words and unreasonable demands. Especially when it came to Hayes.

Hayes had never really understood why his dad had seemed to turn against him, in particular. He wasn't even the oldest. But whatever the reason, Lionel had picked out his middle son as the one to pile the heaviest load of resentment on.

No, Lionel had never laid an angry hand on any of his kids. But he was harsh with his words, and he was merciless with his rules, and he never let up with that behavior once he started.

So Hayes had left as soon as he had his high school diploma.

Blinking, he looked down at the key in his hand and realized he'd been standing there by his parked truck for a few minutes at least, just staring off into space, lost in the past.

He locked the doors with his key fob then turned and jogged back to the building.

An hour later, the ER doctor diagnosed Lionel with acute pancreatitis caused by gallstones. He needed immediate laparoscopic surgery to remove his gallbladder.

As the nurses got to work prepping the old man, Hayes slipped outside to take a call from Braden.

The first words out of Braden's mouth were, "I'm at the ranch. Nobody's here except a great big hairy dog that will not let me in the yard—and brother, I have to tell you. The homeplace looks a lot worse than when I left two months ago. What is going on?"

In spite of how bad things were, Hayes almost smiled. "The dog is mine—and you came, after all."

"I'm not staying long," Braden grumbled.

"Fair enough. And here's the thing…" Hayes quickly filled his brother in on the situation.

"That sounds bad."

"It is. It's serious."

"Are you sure he's going to make it?" Braden spoke in a hushed voice.

"Are you kidding? He's too ornery to roll over and die."

Braden grunted. "You got it right about that."

"I should go back in."

"Rylee there?" Braden asked.

"She was at some sales meeting up in Great Falls when Mom called her. But she should be here soon."

"Good. I'm on my way."

Rylee and her fiancée, Shep Dalton, showed up before they wheeled Lionel into surgery. The old man was pretty out of it by then. He spoke gently to Rylee, which lifted Hayes's spirits a little. Lionel was capable of kindness to his daughter, at least. Maybe there was hope for the old man, after all.

They all four—Norma, Rylee, Shep and Hayes—sat out in the waiting area, hoping for good news. After a tense half hour or so, a nurse emerged to inform them that the simpler, less-invasive laparoscopic surgery wasn't going to do the job. Lionel required an open surgery.

"Doctor Bristol will fill you in on the details later." The nurse spoke directly to Norma then. "Your husband will be in the OR for another hour at a minimum but be prepared for two."

"Is he okay?" Norma asked in a tiny voice.

The nurse gave her a nod and a firm, "Yes. He's in good hands."

Rylee put her arm around their mother and whispered something in her ear.

Norma said, "I know, I know. You're right, honey. Your dad's a tough one."

They all nodded at that, even Shep.

"I hate this," whispered Norma.

Rylee tightened her arm around their mom, hugging her closer as Norma reached out a hand for Hayes. He took it. Shep took Rylee's free hand.

For a while they just sat there, the four of them, no one saying a word, holding on to each other for dear life.

That evening, Chrissy Hastings left the inn a few minutes early. She longed to go home to her cute little condo on First Street, to fix herself a simple dinner of pasta and salad, maybe stream something on Netflix and try not to think about Hayes Parker, which was going to take serious effort. Because Hayes, in his worn boots and weathered Stetson, remained as lean, tall and broad-shouldered as ever. Even his faded jeans fit him the way no jeans had a right to do.

And so much for not thinking about Hayes.

With a weary sigh, she got into her Chevy Blazer and headed for her parents' house. Because when she'd begged off on dinner with them last week, she'd promised she'd be there for the evening meal tonight.

Five minutes later, she was pulling up to the curb in front of the meticulously maintained Craftsman-style bungalow where she'd grown up.

Her mom, Patrice, was waiting at the front door in crisp jeans and a red Western shirt. "There you are! Come in, come in." She grabbed Chrissy close in a too-tight hug. Chrissy breathed in the familiar flowery scent of her mom's favorite perfume. The smell of that perfume made her feel equal parts cherished and smothered. "Your father's in the living room…"

"How's my girl?" Her dad folded his copy of the *Billings Gazette* and set it on the arm of his worn leather chair. "So good to see you." He got up and gave her a hug.

She hugged him back good and hard. Her dad owned Hastings Tractor and Supply right there in town. He sold farm machinery, tools and fencing, along with clothing and anything else you might need to keep your farm or ranch going. He was highly respected, and for good reason. Mel Hastings was kind, thoughtful, patient and helpful. He was also a longtime town councilman.

As for her mom, Patrice was good as gold, yet somehow she always managed to get on Chrissy's last nerve.

Tonight was no exception. They no sooner sat down to dinner than her mom started in.

"Sweetheart, I got a postcard from Sam!" her mom announced gleefully. Sam Shaw was Chrissy's ex-husband. Patrice had always adored Sam. "He says he's doing really well down there in Key West. He says he hopes we're all fine." She leaned in. "Sweetheart, in my heart I just know he misses home—and you."

Chrissy had explained a hundred times that she and Sam had had fertility issues and Sam couldn't deal with that. And so, in the end, they divorced. But her mom still didn't get it—not why Sam would leave her *or* why in the world he would want to go live on a boat in Florida.

"Oh, sweetheart. I just know that someday soon, he will be coming back to you."

Chrissy passed the platter of air-fried chicken thighs to her dad. "Mom, Sam always liked you a lot. It's nice that he sent you a note. But he and I are divorced. It's over between us."

Patrice gave her a look of infinite patience and a sad little sigh. "Of course. You're right. I'm sorry to bring it up."

Chrissy put on a smile. "This chicken looks amazing."

"It's the best," said her dad.

"Life just…moves on so fast these days," said Patrice. "I mean, you and Sam are divorced. And here *you* are, back in town, working at the inn…" She puffed out her cheeks with a hard breath, as though life were just too convoluted for her to comprehend. "I can't keep up with all the changes, with Sam off in Florida *finding* himself or some such. And what about you, going off to one of those tattoo parlors to get words written on your arm that will never wash off?"

Patience, Chrissy thought. "Come on, Mom," she replied in a mild tone. "Enough about the tattoo." Patrice had burst into tears the first time she saw it. "I thought you said you were over it."

"Well, sweetheart, it's only that it really is so...*permanent*, isn't it?" Chrissy said nothing. The silence went on for several seconds. Finally, Patrice added sheepishly, "Though the sentiment is, er, lovely, sweetie. It truly is."

"Thank you, Mom." For no reason whatsoever, Chrissy thought of Hayes right then. Today, he'd looked older and just possibly wiser. But he still had that smoking hot intensity in those green eyes of his.

As though Patrice had the power to read her daughter's mind, she said, "I suppose you've heard already that Hayes Parker is back in town. I ran into Millie Stafford at the grocery store. She said she saw him driving down Central Avenue in a big, black crew cab with a horse trailer hooked on behind…"

Chrissy stifled an eye roll. "Word does get around fast in this town."

Her mom peered at her sharply. "You knew already that he was here, didn't you?"

Why lie? Her mom would know it if she did. "Yeah, I knew. Hayes stopped at the inn this afternoon." When her mom just looked at her, waiting, Chrissy added, "We spoke for maybe a minute and a half. You know, *Hi, how are you? Have a nice life.* He has a beautiful dog. Her name is Rayna." It could be spelled different ways in different languages. But it meant *queen*—and yeah, she'd looked it up. So what?

Patrice sipped her iced tea. "Well, it's no secret that the Parker ranch is in trouble. And now both Braden and Miles are gone. And Millie also mentioned that Lionel isn't doing well. He's been sick a lot lately."

Chrissy nodded. "Hayes did say that Lionel was ill."

"There you have it, then. *Somebody* had to come help out." Patrice shook her head. "Poor Norma. She must be at her wit's end…"

There was more in that vein. Chrissy tuned her mom out. Her mind wandered to thoughts of Hayes, back in Tenacity all over again, having to deal with his sick father, who'd been the reason he left town in the first place.

Forty-five minutes after the nurse came and told them that Lionel needed open gallbladder surgery, Braden appeared. Norma let out a cry at the sight of him and grabbed him in a hug. They brought him up to speed on Lionel's surgery and then they all settled in to wait for the doctor to come and tell them how bad things were.

An hour after that, Dr. Bristol finally came out to report that Lionel was out of surgery and resting comfortably.

"Can we see him?" asked Hayes's mom.

The doctor nodded. "One at a time and very briefly."

Hayes went in third, after his mom and Braden. His dad was pretty out of it—which at least meant that Lionel didn't have the energy to say anything mean. Hayes patted his hand and said, "I'm heading back to the ranch in a bit to handle evening chores."

The old man gave a slow nod. "Good." He said the word so quietly, Hayes had to bend close to hear him. "Real good…"

Hayes went back to the waiting room and Rylee took her turn with their dad.

When Hayes dropped into the chair next to his mom, she said, "They're wheeling a bed into his room for me so that I can stay with him overnight—and for as long as he has to be here."

Hayes wasn't surprised. When his mom put her mind to

something—like sharing her sick husband's hospital room—
she usually managed to make it happen. Norma Parker was
also a saint. She loved her husband through thick and thin,
unconditionally and with her whole heart. Enough to spend
her nights on a rollaway just to stay by his side. "Okay,
Mom. I'll see to things at the ranch."

She eased her hand around his arm and rested her head
against his shoulder. "Thank you, Hayes. It's good to have
you home. I just wish you were here under better circum-
stances."

"Don't we all, Mom," said Braden, who was sitting on
Norma's other side.

Hayes and Braden hung around until Rylee and Shep
went home, and their mom was settled in with Lionel. By
then it was getting pretty late.

The brothers walked out to the parking lot together.
In the bright light beaming down on them from the LED
lamps overhead, Hayes thought Braden looked older than
his thirty-five years.

Hayes knew what his brother was thinking. "Go." Hayes
clapped him on the shoulder. "It's okay."

Braden shook his head. "I'll go back to the ranch with
you, help with the chores, stay the night."

"If you do that, you'll never leave."

They stared at each other. Finally Braden said, "Well,
it *is* your turn."

"Damn right it is." Hayes said it with conviction, though
they both knew coming back to Tenacity was the last thing
he'd ever planned to do.

"Listen, Hayes. I mean this. I want you to call me if
there's—"

"You know I will."

Braden stretched out his long arms. "Get over here."

They shared a quick hug and some back-slapping.

Five minutes later, Braden was gone, and Hayes climbed in his crew cab for the drive back to the ranch.

When he got there, he found Rayna waiting in front of the house. She was still inside the fence. He told her what a good girl she was, giving her plenty of scratches and strokes. Then he fed her. For himself, he heated up some leftovers he found in the fridge. Once he'd straightened up the kitchen, he went outside again and headed for the barn to see what needed doing.

No surprise, it was a lot.

He was up past midnight feeding stock, putting at least a few escaped cattle back behind fences where they belonged and taking care of various other chores that should have been done long ago. He hadn't gotten anywhere near checking the books on his dad's old computer yet, but even in the middle of the night, with the moon beaming down on him, making everything softer and prettier, it was still painfully obvious that the End of the Road Ranch was in deep trouble.

At 12:45 a.m. when he finally climbed the stairs and settled, exhausted, into his narrow childhood bed, he couldn't get to sleep. As he rolled over on his back and stared up at the shadows on the ceiling, he reminded himself that nobody ever said ranch life was easy.

He crawled from the bed at five and headed out to tackle the morning chores—and to discover an even longer list of repairs and neglected tasks that had to be done yesterday.

At ten a.m., he knocked off, took a quick shower and drove into town to drop off the room key he'd never used. He was at the inn for maybe ten minutes total. The whole time he kept expecting to see Chrissy again, anticipating the moment when he'd turn around and find himself look-ing right into those big brown eyes.

That moment came just as he was leaving. He spotted her over by a potted ficus tree, discussing something with a tall, skinny guy—a hotel employee judging by his maroon slacks and vest. She glanced over and saw Hayes looking at her.

He nodded. She nodded back—and then she resumed her conversation with the other man.

Hayes went out the glass doors feeling lonely, wonder-ing what might have happened if she'd had a minute to chat with him.

Outside, he shook his head at his own damn foolish-ness. What did he and Chrissy Hastings have to say to each other anyway? Nothing, that's what. He hardly knew her anymore.

Back at the ranch, he found his mom in the kitchen put-ting groceries in the fridge. "I ran into an old friend up at the hospital and I hitched a ride home with her to pick up the Suburban."

He teased, "Same Suburban you've been driving since before I left town?"

"That's right. It runs great and gets the job done and I'm holding on to it. We stopped at the grocery store in Bronco. I bought enough food to keep you from starving."

"That's all just for me?"

"Hon, I'm going back up to be with your father."

Hayes wasn't surprised. "How's he doing?"

"Well, he's not happy being stuck in the hospital…"

"Translation, he's crabby and short-tempered."

His mother granted him a gentle, accepting smile. "Doc-tor Bristol says your father will be staying right there at Bronco Valley Hospital for the next five or six days, mini-mum."

And there was more. It would be six to eight weeks before Lionel would be able to get around comfortably.

Norma went on, "Doctor Bristol says we have to be realistic. Given your dad's age and how sick he's been, it's going to be quite a while before he'll be out herding livestock and mending fences. How about a big, fat roast beef sandwich with my special potato salad?"

"Thanks, Mom. That sounds amazing."

"Hayes, I am sorry," she said when they sat down to eat. "I should stick around today, take care of my garden, thaw some of the meat in the deep freeze and do some cooking for you. I should give you a hand with the mountain of work that has to be done around here, but I—"

"You need to be with Dad right now. Mom, I understand. I really do. I'm not an eighteen-year-old fool anymore. Dad needs you. As for me, I'll figure things out around here just fine."

She reached across the old pine table and put her hand on his. "You're a good son. The best. Your dad was always too hard on you. I love that man with all my heart, but he really messed up when he drove you away."

"Yes, he did," Hayes said darkly. But then he shrugged. "It was years ago. And we all know I was no saint."

Back then, the tougher Lionel was on him, the more Hayes had acted up. Once he'd gone "surfing" on the hood of a friend's pickup. At sixty miles an hour. Another time, he'd broken into the Grizzly Bar at four in the morning and helped himself to a lot of beer. A sheriff's deputy who'd once worked as a cowhand for Lionel had brought Hayes home in disgrace. Worst of all, Hayes was so drunk, he kept falling down any time the deputy let go of him.

And then there was the night he decided to run away after a fight with Lionel. It was cold out. He'd started a fire to keep warm and the wind had come up. A couple of acres had been burned to black ash before he, his dad, his mom, his brothers and his sister, too, had managed to put the fire out.

"Well, your father was too rough on you," his mother said, waving a wedge of dill pickle. "And you rebelled."

"Yes, I did."

"Sometimes I'm afraid you two won't make up before he…" She looked away. Her lips were pressed together, her chin quivering.

"Mom…" Now he was the one reaching across, squeezing *her* hand. "He'll be okay. He's tough."

She faced him then and whispered, "If you hadn't come home when you did yesterday, I never could have gotten him up to Bronco in time."

"You've got friends you can call, and you would've called them. And you could've called 911. Fire and Rescue would have come to deal with him—and anyway, he's getting the care he needs now. He's going to come through this. He's going to be fine."

She sniffed and straightened her shoulders. "You're right. Of course, you are."

Hayes rose and went around the table to her side. "You've got that look…" He held out his hand.

She took it. "Like I need a hug?"

"That would be the one." He pulled her up and wrapped his arms around her. "It will be all right, Mom."

"Yeah," she whispered, holding on tight.

Twenty minutes later, Norma headed back to Bronco. Once she was gone, Hayes called one of his high school buddies. Jake Marshall had been driving the pickup the night Hayes went surfing on the hood.

After they caught up with each other a little, Hayes laid

the truth right out there. "So anyway. I'm back here in Te-nacity because my dad's in the hospital and the End of the Road Ranch is nothing short of a disaster."

Jake chuckled. "Remember you used to call that place the *End of My Rope Ranch*?"

"Yeah, I remember. Because it was—and it still is, now more than ever…" Hayes hesitated. He was working up the gall to beg for help.

But then Jake said, "I'll make a few calls and be there in a bit."

"Man." Hayes swallowed a hard knot of emotion. "Thank you. I owe you."

"You'd do the same for me. See you soon."

Jake wasn't kidding. He showed up an hour later. And with him he had two of their other high school pals, Beck Douglas and Austin O'Connor.

The four of them went to work. By six that evening, they'd contained all the loose chickens, rounded up several head of wandering cattle, fixed a whole bunch of downed fences, cut a field of alfalfa and even repaired the droop-ing sign at the main gate.

Norma had left a couple of rotisserie chickens in the fridge, along with plenty of coleslaw and potato salad. The four men scarfed down the food and then took turns in the shower.

"It's Friday night," announced Austin, once they were all cleaned up and gathered around the kitchen table enjoy-ing a beer. "You all know what that means."

Beck raised his can of Bud. "To the Grizzly!" he toasted.

Jake snickered as he reached down to give Rayna a good scratch around the neck. "Hayes, we've got good news for you."

"I could use a little of that. Lay it on me."

Jake said, "Ten years ago, old man Kelsy sold the Grizzly to a guy named Dale Clutterbuck. Dale has no memory of that time you broke in and guzzled all the beer."

Hayes actually smiled then. "Hold on a minute. Are you saying that the new owner won't shoot me on sight?"

Austin nodded. "That is exactly what he's saying. Finish your Bud. The Grizzly is waiting."

At the Tenacity Inn, Chrissy was working late on what she had begun to think of as the Worst Day Ever in the History of Bad Days.

It was just one near disaster after another at work. The inn was full for once, mostly because of two mini-conventions, one for a local fertilizer company, the other a couples retreat.

The fertilizer group had somehow managed to turn in an incorrect head count. Instead of thirty employees, there were forty. As for the couples retreat, they were an emotional bunch. They huddled together in small groups, many of them crying, talking much too loudly about their personal issues and their unsatisfying sex lives.

Chrissy did her best to keep up with the situation, running herself ragged making sure all the meals and snacks were delicious, attractive and served on time.

Somehow, though, she made it work. She and the inn's small staff managed to get everyone fed and on to the next meeting without any major screwups. Ruby McKinley, who'd moved to town a couple of years after college and worked the front desk, came to Chrissy's rescue more than once, carrying messages back and forth to the kitchen while Chrissy tried to herd one group in and the other out of the main dining space.

By six, all the meals had finally been served. Chrissy

supervised a swift cleanup and left the inn at a little before seven.

Looking forward to a giant glass of wine and a long soak in the bathtub, Chrissy drove straight to her condo on First Street.

But when she let herself in the door, she heard the strangest dripping sound. Bewildered, she stopped just beyond her small entry hall and stared, disbelieving, across the great room to the pretty kitchen area with its white quartz counters, sage green cabinets and beautiful oversized pendant lighting.

Her mind couldn't quite comprehend what she was seeing. Water was falling out of the ceiling…

Chapter Three

It took her a minute or two of standing there, stunned, with her mouth hanging open, to process what she saw.

Disaster.

That's what it was. Complete disaster.

Water flowed down the pendant lights, splashing onto her quartz countertops, spreading out from there, trickling down her gorgeous cabinets, dripping onto her cute little farm-style table, only to flow off of it and pool on the wood floor.

The building was small, containing four condos total, two up, two down. Evidently, the one above hers had an overflowing tub or a burst pipe.

First priority—flip the breaker. Then pack up what she could and get out.

Staying close to the wall, she darted to the side and through the square of hallway to her tiny laundry room. The breaker box was behind the door. She flipped the main switch, and her place went dark, though the small window over the laundry sink let in the early evening light.

Already the ceiling in there had darkened with a spreading water stain. The overhead light fixture was dripping. She pulled out her phone and called the association that managed the shared areas of the building. The call went to voicemail, so she left a harried message with her name and address, along with a brief description of the problem.

After that, well, what could she do but pack fast and get out?

Twenty minutes later, she'd filled two suitcases. Trying not to think of all her pretty things that would never be the same, she darted back into the great room. Moving as fast as she could along the wall, lugging her suitcases, she quickly reached her small foyer. From there it was only a few steps to the front door and escape.

Outside, she found Darren and Lily Kizer, the couple who owned the other downstairs condo. They stood huddled together, luggage and overflowing boxes waiting at their feet. Her neighbors looked as shell-shocked as Chrissy felt. Unfortunately, the guy who lived in the condo with the leak was nowhere to be seen.

"I went up there and knocked," Darren said. "I knocked hard and for a long time. Nobody answered."

Just then, the guy from the building management company drove up. Ten minutes later, he'd turned off the water and the power to the building and advised Chrissy and her fellow condo owners to call their insurance companies and arrange to stay elsewhere for now.

Lily dared to ask, "How long can we expect to be sleeping *elsewhere*?"

The man from the management company had no idea, but hedged a guess that it could be a while.

"Contact your insurance company ASAP—and your agent, too. The insurance company will send an adjuster out to assess the damage and then they should pay up within thirty days. Your agent should help you navigate the whole process. And the sooner you get to work drying things out, the better. You don't want mold and mildew on top of everything else."

Feeling nothing short of numb, Chrissy called her insurance company's hotline. They promised that an adjuster would contact her within the next three days.

"Three days?" She might have screamed those words. "Can't you get someone over here tomorrow?"

The operator made soothing noises but no promises.

Chrissy loaded her suitcases into the back of her Blazer—and then couldn't decide what to do next.

The inn was full, so she couldn't stay there—not that she really wanted to, anyway. She worked there at least forty hours a week and had no desire to sleep there, too.

She could call a friend.

But that seemed unnecessary. Because her mom and dad would be happy to have her stay with them tonight. And realistically, she was going to end up with them for the next several weeks anyway.

Chrissy cringed at the thought. Several weeks at her mom's house, sleeping in her childhood bedroom, listening to her mom's well-meaning never-ending advice. Did it get any grimmer than that?

Sometimes life just sucked.

Resigned, she got in behind the wheel, started the engine—and then let her head drop to the steering wheel. Sleeping at her mom's house…

No. She simply could not face that yet.

Maybe a drink would help—possibly two. Chrissy rarely drank. But tonight, she needed a little good cheer before making herself deal with her mother's relentless concern for her life and her future. Straightening in her seat, she put on her seat belt and eased out of her parking space behind her building.

At the Grizzly Bar on Central Avenue, warm light spilled from the windows on either side of the orange door. She could hear laughter and honky-tonk music coming from inside.

Her spirits lifted a little. A drink at the Grizzly. Just what she needed, lots of people around her having a good time. Was a good time contagious? She hoped so.

A block down from the bar, she found a parking space. Jumping out of the Blazer, she settled her purse strap on her shoulder and followed the sounds of laughter and music back to the saloon with the orange door.

Inside, the laughter was louder and so was the jukebox. Everyone seemed to be talking at once. Several people were shouting.

She felt a bit foolish, still dressed for work in her white shirt, maroon vest and skirt with practical pumps to match. Well, too bad. She'd had no time to change, given the immediate problem of grabbing her things and getting out before the flood brought a section of ceiling down on her head.

About then, she spotted Hayes, sitting in a corner booth with three of his buddies from high school. He locked eyes on her a second after she saw him.

Their gazes held and Chrissy wanted to throw her head back and scream her frustration at the antler chandelier overhead. She couldn't even have a drink at the local honky-tonk without running into the one man in town she really would rather avoid.

This was simply not her day or night. She wanted to spin on her heel and head right back out the way she'd come in.

But no. Her distressingly hot first love was not driving her out of the Grizzly. At least not until she'd had a drink to fortify herself against the reality of her current situation.

She scanned the packed room. There had to be a seat

for her somewhere—and then she saw it. There was one empty stool at the bar.

Luck was with her for once, and she got there before anyone else did. She climbed on that stool with a sigh of relief and hung her shoulder bag on the convenient hook down by her knees.

The big, bearded guy behind the bar came right over. "Welcome to the Grizzly. I'm Dale."

She recognized him. "Dale Clutterbuck, right? The owner."

Dale's smile was contagious. "That's me."

She offered her hand. He took it. "I'm Chrissy Hastings," she said.

"Mel's daughter, right?"

"You got it."

"What can I get for you, Chrissy?"

"Margarita, please."

Dale served her and headed back down the bar to fill other orders.

Chrissy drank half her margarita in two sips. It didn't help much. She still felt like bursting into tears of misery and frustration. But she kept a big smile on her face, sipped again and promised herself that she wasn't going to get weepy. She would drink her two-drink limit—slowly—and eventually she would feel ready to head for her folks' place.

A hand closed on her shoulder.

She stiffened and slowly turned her head. Now she was looking into the bloodshot eyes of a guy she'd never seen before. Clearly intoxicated, he gave her a woozy smile. "Hey there, gorgeous. Where you been all my life?"

"Take your hand off my shoulder please," she replied in a voice of velvet over steel.

It worked. The drunk let go of her shoulder. But he didn't step back. "Listen. I'm here and so're you." Breathing ninety proof, he leaned in even closer. "What does that tell you, baby?"

"That I suddenly wish I was somewhere else?"

The drunk scowled. "Huh?"

It was exactly the wrong response after Chrissy's terrible, awful, endless day. She took her purse off the hook, spun on the stool and faced him directly. "Sometimes when you see a woman alone it's because being alone is exactly what she wants."

The guy leaned closer and sneered, "Pretty lady, you got a bad attitude."

She clutched the strap of her purse tightly in one hand just in case she had to fend him off with it and matched her annoyance to his. "And you can't take a hint. Let me be perfectly clear. Leave. Me. Alone."

About then, she realized that the Grizzly had gone pin-drop quiet.

Down the bar, Dale called out to the drunk man who wouldn't go away. "What'd I tell you, Roger? Time to head on home!"

Roger sneered. "I got no wheels. You know that."

"It's not that far. Call a friend to come and get you, or start walkin'."

Roger grunted and held his ground. Worse, he grabbed Chrissy's arm.

Hayes had been trying his best not to let his gaze wander in Chrissy's direction. But he'd known from the moment she came through the orange door that something was wrong. Yeah, it had been forever since she was his girl, but still. He'd known her so well. She might be all grown up now, but she was still Chrissy.

And tonight, for whatever reason, she was not happy.

When she first came in, their eyes had met for just those few seconds. Then she looked away and didn't look back.

He got the message. She was miserable. But as far as she was concerned, that was none of his business and he should leave her alone.

So he had.

Until now. Because no way could he let some drunk fool get up in her face like that—and worse, put his hands on her.

Hayes slid from the booth.

"Hayes, you want backup?" asked Beck.

He shook his head. "I got this."

He took two steps and then paused as Chrissy got down off her stool, drew herself up to her full five foot, seven inch height and smiled with her teeth showing. Pulling up even taller, she whispered something in the drunk's ear.

The drunk blinked and jerked back like she'd slapped him. "What'd you say?" he growled as he let go of her arm.

She leaned right toward the guy again and whispered some more.

Whatever she said worked. Roger put up both hands and backed away three steps. And then, staggering a bit, he turned and went out the orange door.

When the door swung shut behind him, the dead-quiet bar erupted in applause. There was also whistling and a number of shouts of "way to go" in appreciation and respect for the way Chrissy had shut the drunk down.

In response to the applause, Chrissy put on her biggest, brightest smile. Yeah, Hayes knew that smile was fake. But it dazzled him, nonetheless. Finally, still smiling, Chrissy took a bow.

By then, Hayes was at her side. He asked quietly, "You okay?"

"I am just fine." She smiled on through gritted teeth.

"Look, let me buy you a drink and we can—"

"Maybe some other time." She said it softly, gently. He could see it was taking all the will she possessed to keep her brave smile in place. "I have to go." She hooked her purse on her shoulder. "You take care, Hayes." And she started for the door.

Hayes glanced toward the table where his friends waited. He tipped his head toward Chrissy's retreating back. They got the message and remained in the booth. Chrissy went out the door. Beck tossed him his hat as he passed them. Settling it on his head, he followed Chrissy from the bar.

By then, it was dark out. The Central Avenue street-lights had come on. Hayes just stood there on the sidewalk for a moment, hanging back. Chrissy was halfway across the street by then, probably headed for the bus-stop bench in its plexiglass shelter. When she got there, she dropped to the bench, pressed her knees together, braced her fore-arms on her lap and stared at the sidewalk beneath her feet.

Still, he lingered by the orange door, watching over her from a distance just in case Roger reappeared. Eventually, Chrissy looked up and spotted him. For several seconds, she glared defiantly at him.

And then, blowing out her cheeks as if keeping up the animosity was just too much work, she dropped her gaze and stared down at her shoes again.

He crossed the street. "Mind if I share your bench with you?"

She slanted him one of those are-you-kidding-me looks. But then she sighed. "This bench is public property. I have no say as to who sits on it."

He swept off his hat. "I'm going to take that to mean, 'Sure, Hayes. Have a seat.'"

She gave him a dramatic eye roll, but she didn't object, so he sat as far away from her as the bench allowed and put his hat in his lap.

Neither of them spoke for several minutes.

Eventually, a guy came out of the Grizzly and headed down the street whistling. Two women emerged, laughing, their arms around each other. They went the other way.

Hayes dared to slide a glance at Chrissy just as she snuck a quick look at him. Tears gleamed in her eyes.

Angrily, she swiped them away. "I don't know what I'm doing," she said, her voice low enough he had to lean her way to hear it. "My parents adored my ex-husband and sometimes I think that my mother still doesn't really believe that Sam and I are actually divorced. I'm just…well, I mean, I'm figuring things out slowly, but some days are hard. Today was the worst ever." She tipped her head to the sky and let out a groan. "Oh, why am I telling you all this?" she moaned.

"Hey," he suggested gently. "It's okay. I'm here and I'm willing to listen."

She laughed, but it wasn't a happy sound.

And then she turned those big brown eyes directly on Hayes. He felt that look like a shock of electricity shooting right through him. "That guy in the bar…?"

"Yeah?"

"He scared me."

"He was an ass, and you took care of him just fine."

She giggled then, wrinkling her nose at him like she had a secret at the same time as her eyes looked so sad. "Want to know how I backed that sucker off?"

"You bet I do."

"I confessed in graphic terms to having an STD."

He almost burst out laughing, but somehow he managed to play it straight. "Impressive."

"Thank you—but for a minute there, I didn't know what would happen. He freaked me out. It's just…my life, you know?"

"No, Chrissy. I don't know. What about your life?"

"My life is one disaster after another."

"Maybe it just seems that way today."

"Hayes. It *is* that way. Just take my word for it."

"All right. But I'm saying it again. What you did in there was perfect."

"Thank you," she replied in a small voice.

He shrugged. "It's only the truth."

She gave him a nod and said nothing else. He got it. She still wanted to be left alone. He should go.

But somehow, he couldn't bring himself to leave her sitting there alone.

Chrissy really didn't want to lay all her troubles on her long-ago boyfriend.

But he was here, and he was being so great. And she really needed to talk to someone.

And so, sitting at the bus stop across from the Grizzly at nine thirty on that warm August night, Chrissy told Hayes everything about her terrible, awful, endless day.

It took a while, but he sat there and listened to all of it. He listened like he cared, like it mattered to him that her workday had been its own special kind of hell, that her cute condo was now a disaster zone, and she was about to move in with her parents again.

"Tell you what," he said when she finally fell silent. "Why don't you just come and stay at the ranch? My brothers are gone and my sister lives in Bronco now. That leaves more than one empty bedroom upstairs. You can take your pick."

She looked at him without speaking for a long time. He didn't try to break the silence. Finally, she said, "I couldn't." Although staying at the Parker ranch seemed a lot less depressing than moving in with her parents.

"Why not? I promise you, Chrissy, I'm not going to get in your space or anything." He put up a hand, a witness swearing an oath. "Friends only, you have my word."

"I believe you." And she did, she realized as she said the words. "But won't your parents have something to say about your high school girlfriend moving in with you?"

"Nope. My dad's in the hospital after major surgery and won't be home for a week or so. And my mom made them wheel a bed into his room for her. She won't be home much in the next week or so either—not that it will matter to her. She's always loved you. For now, I'm alone at the house. You might as well use one of those empty rooms."

She set her purse on the bench between them. "I can't believe I'm actually considering it." But she was. Because right now moving in with her long-lost first love felt like a much better option than going back to her parents' house again.

She might be able to get a room at the inn once the weekend was over. But then she'd be living at her place of work, which made her uncomfortable—not to mention it could get expensive.

Who knew how long repairs would take at her place or how much her insurance would end up paying?

Yeah, she and Hayes had a painful history with each other. And he was still one hot cowboy.

Maybe too hot. Maybe that she was even considering staying at the ranch house with him was just asking for trouble.

Hot trouble, she couldn't help thinking.

And then she frowned because…how could she be thinking about having sex with her ex at a time like this?

She was losing it, no doubt about that.

"Look," Hayes said. "If staying at the ranch doesn't work out for you, your parents aren't going anywhere. You can ditch plan B and head for your mom's house."

The more she considered the idea of a room at the ranch, the more appeal it had—Hayes Parker's hotness aside. "I would want to pitch in, help with chores and with meals."

"Works for me. The ranch is a big job. I can use all the help I can get."

"And I would pay for the room."

"No. Uh-uh. You help out with the house, pitch in with groceries, do some cooking, that's more than enough."

"But I—"

He put up a hand to silence her. "Stop. You pitch in. That's enough."

She knew that look in his eye. He would not take her money for the room. "Thank you, Hayes."

For that she got a quick nod. Then he went right on to the next question. "You need to go back to your place tonight?"

She shook her head. "I packed some bags. The good news is I'm not on the schedule at the inn tomorrow or Sunday. So I'll have time this weekend to start dealing with the mess at my condo."

"So then. You have a plan."

"More or less, yes."

He laughed then. The sound was warm and somehow private—just between the two of them. That laugh stirred memories better left alone.

And apparently, Hayes thought so, too. The laugh faded. He asked briskly, "Where are you parked?"

"Up the street."

"I'm in the lot behind the bar. I'll get my crew cab and you can fall in behind me."

"Okay."

He rose. She looked up at him in his worn jeans and black T-shirt. All cowboy, lean and tall and ready for anything— including coming to the rescue of the girl he left behind. He started to turn.

"Hayes?"

"Yeah?"

"I'll say it again. Thank you."

He touched the brim of his hat. "Anytime, Chrissy. You know that."

"Best to take Rylee's room," Hayes suggested, pushing open the door to the bedroom at the end of the upstairs hall. "It's got that window with a view of the mountains—yeah, they're way in the distance, but on a clear night, they look real pretty under the stars." Rylee's room was also the farthest from his room—the one he used to share with Miles back in the day. He figured she'd be more comfortable off to herself.

She caught her lower lip between those pretty white teeth and worried it nervously. "You sure Rylee won't mind me moving her stuff around, taking over her space?"

"Rylee took everything she wanted when she moved to Bronco. It really isn't her room anymore."

"Well, then." Chrissy was nodding. "Okay. I'll take it."

"Great." He carried her suitcases into the room and set them on the blue rug by the bed. "There's only the one bathroom up here. I hope you don't mind sharing."

"No, of course not. This is so great." She tried a teasing smile. "I promise not to hog the bathroom."

"Just make yourself comfortable. I mean that."

"I will—and thank you again."

With a nod, he left her.

Chrissy had more than a little trouble sleeping that night. She worried about her condo. How long would it be before she could move back in? Would her insurance cover all the damage? How much might it end up costing her?

And it wasn't only her ruined condo that kept her awake. She couldn't stop second-guessing her decision to stay here in this house with Hayes sleeping in the room down the hall. It was years ago, what they had. They were kids then. They were two different people now.

But still, it felt so…intimate. The two of them, sharing a house after all this time.

Way past midnight, she finally drifted off. And she woke to her phone's alarm clock, which she'd set for five a.m.

In the bathroom, she splashed water on her face, ran a brush through her hair and secured it in a low ponytail. Back in her room, she dressed in jeans and a pink T-shirt with *Cowgirls don't cry—but you might if you cross one* printed on the front.

Downstairs the coffee was already made. She poured herself a mugful and stood sipping it, staring out the window over the sink. There was a light on in the barn, which meant Hayes was already out doing morning chores.

It would be a few hours before she could try to get hold of her insurance agent and the water damage restoration people, so she ran back upstairs to put on an old pair of sneakers.

A few minutes later, she found Hayes feeding the horses. He said he was on top of things and that his friends would be there in an hour or so.

"Have you gathered the eggs yet?" she asked.

One side of his mouth lifted in a grin. She knew he was remembering the old days. He used to let her gather eggs in the evenings sometimes when she'd come over to hang out with him. Mostly, they tried to stay away from the house because his dad was constantly on his case. Lionel Parker had always treated Chrissy like a queen—and his wife and daughter, too. But he was hard on the boys, Hayes most of all.

"All right," said Hayes. "You go on and gather eggs—and don't let those chickens peck your hands off."

"I won't. I've got a special way with the hens."

He gave a little snort of laughter. "Or so you always said."

Two hours later, she returned to the house ahead of Hayes and started cooking breakfast. She got lucky and found some potatoes in the fridge to brown in a skillet with onions and olive oil. She also fried up enough bacon and sausage and cracked enough eggs for Austin, Beck and Jake, too. The boys had driven up a while ago and gone right to work alongside Hayes.

She was standing at the stove turning the skillet potatoes, expecting the four of them to come in loud and hungry any minute now, when she heard the front door open and close. "Food's ready!" she called out over her shoulder. "And the coffee's fresh!"

Footsteps approached through the great room and stopped stock-still several feet behind her. "Chrissy? My dear, sweet Lord, is that you?"

Chrissy set down the slotted spatula in the spoon rest and turned. "Norma! Hey…"

Norma carried four plastic grocery bags, two hooked on each hand. She dipped and set them on the kitchen floor and then rushed around the high, narrow table that served as a kitchen island to grab Chrissy in a tight, warm hug. "Oh, my heavens," she whispered, tears in her voice. "I never thought I would see you in my kitchen again." Norma's hug got even tighter.

When Hayes's mom let her go, they just stood there staring at each other. Norma's eyes were misty with emotion. Chrissy knew hers were, too.

Then Norma asked in a hushed whisper, "So then, you and Hayes...?"

Chrissy slowly shook her head. "It's not like that." Quickly, she explained about her flooded condo and Hayes's offer of a room at the ranch for as long as she needed it. "So, I'm staying in Rylee's old room as of last night, intending to help out where I can. From what I've been told, dealing with the water damage at my place is going to take a while. So once you bring Lionel home, well, we'll see how it goes."

Norma braced her hands on her generous hips. "And here I was hoping that you two had gotten back together again."

"No," Chrissy said firmly. "He's helping me out and I really appreciate it—as long as you're okay with my staying here, too?"

"Am I *okay* with it? Are you kidding me? I'm so glad to see you here." Norma beamed. "Even if you and Hayes aren't going to be getting back together, it sure is good to have you with us on the ranch again." She rounded the island to grab her grocery bags and started putting stuff away as she explained that she'd left the hospital early to buy groceries so she could stock the fridge. "Now that Hayes's friends are helping out, I want to be sure there's plenty in the pantry to keep their bellies full."

"You must have left Bronco before dawn."

"You know me. I like to get up early and get stuff done."

"But, Norma, it's a lot, driving back and forth from Bronco."

"It's not so bad."

"Listen, I'm going to pitch in with food, too. That way you don't have to make the drive as often."

"Oh, now, sweetie…"

Chrissy held up her slotted spatula for silence. "Don't argue. I have to do something to hold up my end here."

"There's chops, roasts, you-name-it in the deep freeze. And vegetables from my garden, too. Use them."

What could Chrissy say? "Thank you. I will."

"And let me give you some cash for—"

"Absolutely not. Norma, I need to contribute, and you need to let me."

There was more hugging before Chrissy went back to the stove.

The boys came in a couple of minutes later. They drank lots of coffee and shoveled in the food.

During the quick meal, Hayes said, "Chrissy, the boys and me are going to follow you to your place, deal with what we can water-wise and help you get more of your things out of there."

Chrissy shook her head—because no way was that happening. "I'll take care of my place. You guys have way more than enough to do here."

"Come on." Hayes gave her one of those looks of his, the kind that used to have her agreeing to any old thing he wanted her to do. "We can get a lot done," he coaxed. "And we can do it fast."

She stared him square in the eye. "You're letting me stay here. It's way more than enough. I have the whole day off to start getting a handle on the disaster at my place."

"But I—"

"Stop." She pointed a slice of bacon at him. "Thank you, but I've got this."

Hayes let it go. When the men were done eating, they cleared off their places. Then Chrissy and Norma shooed them back out to work.

Once they were gone, Chrissy started loading the dishwasher. She was filling the top rack with coffee mugs when Norma asked, "Don't you have calls to make?"

"I do. And as soon as I clean up the kitchen, I'll—"

"Nope. Uh-uh. I'll take care of the cleanup. You need to get the water out of your condo today if at all possible. You know it doesn't take long for mold and mildew to set in and then all your problems are multiplied."

Chrissy groaned. "You're freaking me out, Norma."

"That is my intention. You need to get on top of the problem." Norma reached around her and shut the dishwasher. Then Hayes's mom took her by the shoulders and turned her away from the kitchen counter. "Now start making calls."

"Fine." Chrissy tried her insurance agent first. A woman answered the phone and promised that Chrissy's agent would call her back within the hour.

The agent reached out fifteen minutes later with numbers for the nearest highly rated water abatement companies—and to tell her she needed to get over to her condo and drain the pipes by turning on all the faucets and repeatedly flushing the toilets. "Wear rubber gloves and boots," he suggested. "I'm guessing it's wet in there."

"No kidding," she muttered.

"You have your list of all your household goods and equipment and their value, right?"

She was able to say yes to that. Her dad was big on being prepared. And when she'd bought and furnished her condo, he'd insisted she make a detailed list of all her things and their value. At the time, she'd thought going to all that trouble was a bit ridiculous. But right now, she kind of wished her dad was at her side so that she could hug him.

Before she headed for her condo, she called the water abatement companies. Both were in Bronco. The first call went to voicemail. An actual human answered the second one. He asked questions about the damage and about her insurance company—because she needed to get the adjuster out immediately so the water damage company could create a plan and submit it for payment.

It all went around in a circle, and she was dizzy just thinking about it. Next, the water abatement guy warned her that mold and mildew would set in within twenty-four to forty-eight hours if she didn't get the water out of her home.

By then she was so frustrated with the impossibility of the task ahead of her that she got snippy with the poor guy. "Yeah, my high school boyfriend's mom already explained about the mold and mildew, thank you."

She hung up. Her last call was to the condo management representative who assured her she was cleared to get back into her unit. The power was still off, but in the daytime, that wouldn't be an issue.

When she told Norma where she was headed, Hayes's mom disappeared down the hall and came back with two big rolling suitcases, rubber gloves and rain boots.

Norma said. "Lionel and I were always planning to go on one of those cruises. Never has happened so far, but at least we bought the luggage. And there are a few duffel-type bags inside these big ones. Whatever you can carry that isn't wet, bring it back here—in fact, wet clothes should be fine too. You can just throw them in the washer. Take some big plastic trash bags to bring them back in."

"Oh, Norma!" Chrissy grabbed the older woman in a fierce hug. "Thank you."

Norma guided a loose swatch of hair behind Chrissy's ear—and said, "I'm coming with you to help."

Chrissy just shook her head. "I'm on it. Don't worry."

Norma clucked her tongue. "Your dad is the one with the clout in this town. He is on the town council, after all. I'm betting he could really get things moving on the water abatement and insurance front. Just call him."

"I will."

Norma still wasn't satisfied. "Do it now." And then she just stood there and waited.

Chrissy gave in and made the call—to the number at her dad's store.

"Tenacity Tractor and Supply. This is Myron." Myron Betts had worked at the store for as long as Chrissy could remember.

"Hey, Myron. It's—"

"Miss Chrissy! How you doing?"

"Just great," she lied with enthusiasm. "Listen, is my dad around?"

"You bet. Hang on."

A moment later, her dad came on the line. "How's my girl?"

Her throat clutched, "Well, Dad, I…" Norma was watching her, those green eyes so much like Hayes's eyes urging her to tell her father everything. She gave in enough to admit, "I've got a big problem."

"Well, I'm glad you called, Sugar Bee." The endearment made her tear up all over again. Her dad had always loved Sugar Bee apples. He'd started calling Chrissy his little Sugar Bee when she was still in diapers. "If you've got a problem," he said, "let's get it solved."

It all came pouring out then—the burst pipe upstairs and all that happened after.

Her dad listened without a single interruption until she said, "That's it. That's my problem."

"Don't you worry for a minute," he instructed. "I get that it's bad. But you and me, we're going to jump right on this problem. I'm not going to promise you it won't take a while, but I'll see to it that everything is good as new without you suffering a big gouge in your savings account. Now, have you got rubber boots and gloves?"

She gave Norma a wobbly smile. "I do, yes."

"Let's get after it then. Where are you?"

She considered trying to bypass that question. Not because her dad would make a big deal of her staying at the Parker place, but because he would tell her mom. There was no predicting how Patrice would respond to the news.

But then, who did Chrissy think she was kidding? It was such a small town. One way or another, her mom would find out where Chrissy was staying.

And that was not in any way a problem for Chrissy, she reminded herself. She was thirty-three years old. Where she slept was her business, and her mom would just have to deal with that.

"I ran into Hayes last night, Dad," she explained. "We struck a deal. I'm staying at the ranch and I'm helping out around the ranch house by way of saying thank you."

"Ah," said her dad. Then he added, "You know you're welcome to stay with us. Your mom would love the chance to fuss over you."

Exactly, Chrissy thought. "Thanks, Dad. But I'm fine at the ranch."

"Well, all right, then." He left it at that, which she greatly appreciated. "Meet you at your condo in twenty minutes?"

"I'll be there."

Her dad showed up at the condo in his big crew cab with a trailer hitched on behind. The two of them put on their rubber boots and gloves and made a quick pass of the rooms in her unit just to get an idea of the damage.

Her dad started making calls. Chrissy flushed the toilets and turned on all the faucets to get the water out of the pipes. After that, she made a couple of trips out to her Blazer for the suitcases and the box of big plastic bags.

The insurance agent, the adjuster and the guy from the water abatement company appeared as she was filling the suitcases and bags. Because when Mel Hastings made the calls, stuff got done.

Around ten, a couple of burly guys from her dad's store showed up with another truck and lots of packing boxes. They carried her furniture out. Some of it was unsalvageable and would go to the dump. Everything else, her dad would keep in his warehouse until her place was back together again.

By late afternoon, Chrissy felt ready to drop. But it had been a very productive day. The water abatement crew had the standing water cleared out. Every window was open. They had their own generators in their enormous truck to run all of their equipment—including high-powered blower fans to speed up the drying process.

Also, the condo management company had contacted the owner of the unit above Chrissy's. Another abatement crew had worked up there for most of the day. From them, Chrissy's dad had learned that most of the building's walls and ceilings would have to be ripped out to the studs and replaced. Chrissy knew she wouldn't be moving back in for a while.

Late that afternoon, when Chrissy hugged her dad and

thanked him repeatedly, he kissed the top of her head and promised her everything was going to work out fine.

"Just give it time," he whispered. "And call your mother," he added before he let her go. She promised she would.

Chrissy waited until she was back at the ranch to make the call. Stopping by the rail fence next to the front gate, she turned off the engine and dialed her mom's number right there in her Blazer before she went inside.

Her mom answered on the first ring. "Sweetheart, I've been worried sick. How are you?"

"It's okay, Mom. Really. I'm fine. And I'm guessing Dad filled you in on the disaster at my condo?"

"Oh, yes, he did. I'm so glad you called him."

"Me too. He got right on it. He's the greatest."

"Sweetheart, why don't you come on home and stay with us until you can get back into your condo? Your old room is ready and waiting for you."

She'd known that was coming. And she had her answer ready. "I have a place to stay, Mom. But thank you for offering."

Right then, the front door opened, and Hayes emerged wearing his usual worn jeans and dark T-shirt. His thick brown hair looked wet. No doubt he'd just jumped in the shower after a long day of mending fences and feeding stock. She stuck her hand out her window and gave him a quick wave.

He came down the steps toward her, all lean, easy grace. True, they were over as a couple and had been for years and years. But looking at him now, well, she couldn't fault her younger self for falling head-over-heels for the guy. Even now, her breath came faster just at the sight of him.

Her mom said, "I want you to come home, sweetie. Let me spoil you a little."

"Thank you, truly. But I'm all set up at—"

Patrice cut her off. "I know. Your father told me. End of the Road Ranch."

Hayes came out through the gate, his big dog right behind him. A moment later, he stood by her open window, looking like the best kind of trouble, waiting for her to finish on the phone.

Her mom was still talking. "…because there is no reason for you to stay with the Parkers when you can—"

"Mom. Let's not do this. I'm staying at the Parker ranch and it's working out fine." Hayes raised an eyebrow at her through the open window. She wrinkled her nose at him, then held up her index finger and mouthed, *One minute.* He nodded.

Her mother asked, "But are you sure that's a good idea?"

"Yes, I am. And I have made my decision on this. So let's just leave this subject behind, all right?"

"You are so stubborn."

"I love you, Mom. Lots. But I really have to go now."

"Well, if you change your mind—"

"I won't. But thank you."

"Listen, I'll have dinner on the table in half an hour. Why don't you just come on over and eat. Then you can hang out here for a little while. I would love to see you."

"Sorry, Mom. I can't tonight."

"Soon, then?"

"Yes. I promise. And I have to go. Bye, now." She disconnected the call before her mom could pile on more pressure. "Whew." She dropped the phone on the dashboard.

Hayes leaned in the window, bringing the clean scent of soap from his recent shower. His mouth had that sexy quirk at the corner and those green eyes glittered. She smiled at him, her breath kind of tangling up on her chest. The man was a menace in the best kind of way. He asked, "Bad day?"

"Hellacious. But also extremely productive, so I'm not complaining."

"Well, I'm glad you got a lot done."

"Yes, we did."

He was eyeing the duffel bags piled on the passenger seat as well as the suitcases, carryalls and plastic bags in back. "Let's get all this stuff inside."

"Sounds good. Then I'll get going on dinner."

He grinned again. "Dinner's handled."

"What?"

"There's no need for you to cook tonight."

Chrissy smiled in exhausted delight. "Wait. Don't tell me. Your mom cooked before she left."

He nodded. "Meat loaf, mashed potatoes, green beans with bacon. Cornbread, too."

She put her hand over her heart. "I love your mom so much."

"She's a wonder. No doubt about it." He pulled open her door and gestured her out with a flourish.

"Why, thank you," she said, playing it just a little bit coy.

"For you, anything."

Chrissy got out and knelt to greet Rayna who wagged her giant, furry tail at the attention. "The guys?"

"They took off already." He opened the rear driver's-side door and started pulling out bags.

Working together, it didn't take them long to get everything inside. They piled most of the duffels and suitcases in Braden's old room and carried the plastic bags of wet clothes and linens to the laundry room off the kitchen.

Once he brought the last suitcase in, she said, "I'm going to get a load of laundry going and then I really need a shower."

He gave her one of those smiles that seemed so off-hand and casual—and yet still managed to have her feeling a little bit giddy. He was truly that kind of man—the dangerous kind. The kind that got her all stirred up with just that bad-boy grin of his and the knowing gleam in his eyes. "Go for it," he said, that smile of his somehow managing to get even sexier.

They'd agreed they were just friends and yet here he was, outright flirting with her. She should tell him to knock it off. But she didn't.

It wasn't until she was naked in the shower that she started to reevaluate her own reactions to Hayes.

Because really, she needed to watch herself.

She'd been in love with him once—deeply. Passionately. And he'd shattered her nineteen-year-old heart into a thousand pieces, laying down that ultimatum the way he had.

Marry me, he'd demanded. *Marry me now, or it's over.*

She didn't even like to think about how awful it had been to lose him. It had taken a long time to put herself back together again after Hayes Parker finished stomping on her heart.

She couldn't afford to let herself get worked up over him now. Her heart had been broken twice already. A third break might just finish her off. Yes, it was so kind of him to give her a place to stay when she really needed one.

But she had no business letting herself get too close or too friendly with him. She couldn't go getting all hot and bothered over his devilish grin or his lean, hard body or the smell of his aftershave.

Please. She was smarter than that now.

Quickly, she finished her shower. Leaving her damp hair to air dry, she toweled off fast and pulled on clean clothes.

When she joined Hayes in the kitchen, he turned from

the counter by the fridge where he had the food dished up and ready for reheating in the microwave. He met her eyes.

And she knew that *he* knew. He saw that she had her guard back up.

That warm, teasing smile of his died on his lips.

And all of a sudden, she just felt sad. Drained. Exhausted from a long day's work—and let down, too. Because getting dangerously close to flirting with him earlier? She had loved it. Even though she knew it was flirting with disaster.

He asked, "You okay?"

She nodded. "Just tired, that's all."

"I get it, Chrissy. I really do."

They stood there in silence a few feet apart and stared at each other. Over by the table, Rayna whined, an anxious sound.

And then Hayes said, low and intently, "Just friends."

She nodded. "That's right."

"Look, Chrissy. I'm sorry if I—"

She didn't let him finish. "There is nothing you need to apologize for. You've been so terrific, helping me out the way you have. I'm grateful. And surprisingly, given the awful way things ended for us back in the day, I just, well, this isn't going as I expected. I didn't think it would be so easy to, um, like you again."

"I hear you. And I… I like you, too." He said it kind of bleakly.

She pressed her hands to her cheeks. They felt warm. She wasn't sick, so she must be blushing. Which was unacceptable. She ordered the blush to fade, dropped her arms to her sides and spoke carefully. "After the way it ended for us, I just didn't imagine how natural it would be to, you know, joke around with you, to have fun just being with you."

His nod was slow. Thoughtful. "Yeah. It's the same for

me. So easy and natural…" His words trailed off. And then he added in a brisk tone, "So then, let's eat?"

She allowed herself a smile. "Yes, please."

Chapter Four

For the next few days, Hayes took extra care to give Chrissy her space.

Because she was right. They had to be careful around each other. They needed to avoid getting overly friendly.

The thing was, he did like her. A lot. Her face and body held the same magnetic appeal for him as back in high school.

And damn. Was she ever smart. That drunk at the Grizzly Friday night had not stood a chance against that quick wit of hers. With just a few choice words, she'd had him staggering out the door.

Hayes shook his head, grinning, remembering the past.

Back in high school, all the guys had liked her. And it wasn't only the way she looked that made her beautiful. It was also her goodness. Chrissy Hastings was one of those people who would always offer help and a kind word when either was needed. He'd known her since grade school and the two of them had always been friendly.

But by freshman year, she'd changed. She came back to school with curves and a womanly way about her. That first day back, she'd smiled at him—a special smile that told him she was seeing him in a new light, too. That smile had made him the happiest guy at Tenacity High. Within a week, they were holding hands in the hallways, meeting up between classes, inseparable. He'd believed they were forever.

Looking back, it still came to him vividly, how angry and hurt he'd been when she refused to marry him. He'd been furious at her then—for promising to love him forever, for making him believe in her. And then turning her back on him when things got too tough. Back then, he'd had his butthurt blinders on. Because he was nineteen and his forever love had walked away.

However, right now, as a grown man, he saw her choice in a whole different light. He realized he'd let the chip on his shoulder drive her away.

Hayes had wanted her to leave town with him.

She wouldn't. But she hadn't dumped him. After he left, she'd remained his girl long-distance.

For almost a year, he called her often, begging her to join him at the ranch down near Kaycee, Wyoming, where he'd hired on as a cowhand.

She'd loved him, she really had—loved him as much as he'd loved her. And finally, during her spring break in her freshman year at Montana State, she came to visit him.

As soon as he had his arms around her again, Hayes had taken her hand, slipped a gold ring with an itty-bitty diamond on her finger and asked her to marry him. She balked. She tried to make him see that she just wasn't ready for marriage. That they were both too young—and he lived in a tiny old trailer provided by his boss.

He remembered her standing by the rusty sink in that rickety trailer, begging him to try to see it her way...

"Hayes, won't you please try to understand? There's no room for me here. I love you. You know I do. And I don't

*see why we can't stay together long-distance. I promise
I'm yours and I always will be. But I can't come live with
you now. And really, it won't be so bad. We can visit each
other every chance we get."*

He saw red then. He was through with her telling him no.

*Drawing his shoulders back, he stood tall. He wasn't
having less than all of her—all of her, right now. "It's not
enough, Chrissy. Marry me."*

*Those big brown eyes begged him and so did that soft
mouth of hers. "Oh, Hayes, please try to understand. I can't.
Please won't you wait for me? At least let me finish college
before we go talking about getting married?"*

*He'd scoffed in her face. "Be with me. Now. Marry me.
Or we're done."*

Twenty minutes later, he'd watched her drive away.

He'd hated her then. And for the next five years or so,
he'd burned with fury every time he thought of her. Even
when he met Anna and found himself wanting to get to
know her better, he'd continued to think of Chrissy with
fury in his heart.

That anger didn't fade until about the time he admitted
to himself that he was ready to try love again—with the
boss's daughter.

Looking back, he could see now how similar Anna was
to Chrissy. Both of them were big-hearted and smart, quick
to laugh and to find the joy in life. Anna was a rancher's
daughter. Her dad had put her on a horse when she was
barely out of diapers. Chrissy was a town girl. But deep
down they were both strong women who knew what they
wanted and went after it. He'd been happy with Anna, and
he'd put Chrissy behind him.

Or so he'd thought.

But now, Anna was gone forever.

And the last thing he'd ever expected was to find himself sharing a home with Chrissy at the End of the Road Ranch and liking her a little too much, realizing that she was every bit as strong, smart and desirable as she'd been at nineteen.

Even more so if the truth were told.

He needed to watch himself around her. It would be far too easy to start hoping for more than either of them were ready for at this point in their lives.

Austin, Jake and Beck showed up bright and early on Sunday. Chrissy cooked them all breakfast and then went off to work at the inn.

That evening, she got back to the ranch at five. Hayes's friends had gone home. It was just the two of them at the dinner table. She served spaghetti with meat sauce, garlic bread and a big green salad and then sat there eating in silence, strangely afraid that anything she might say would be overly friendly, somehow.

After several endless minutes of quiet interrupted only by the sound of Rayna's tags rattling as she scratched herself and the scrape of forks on plates, Chrissy took a stab at conversation. "So how was your day?" she asked, knowing it was arguably the most boring question ever. But hey. At least she'd tried.

He swallowed pasta and knocked back a big gulp of water. "Nothing special. We burned a bunch of ditches, baled the hay we cut on Friday and whitewashed a couple of sheds."

"Wow. That's a lot." She tried to think what else to say as he nodded and shoveled in another forkful of spaghetti. "At this rate, you'll have the ranch in tiptop shape in no time."

He scoffed at that. "Doubtful." And he forked up a big bite of salad.

As she watched him chew, she realized he really didn't want to chat with her and she might as well give up trying to get a conversation going.

Hayes kept eating. He plowed through that meal at the speed of light. As soon as he'd devoured his second helping of pasta and meat sauce, he was on his feet. "I'm going to get after the evening chores. I'll probably be a while."

"All right."

"The baler needs a little housekeeping. It's been running hot, and I should probably blow out the oil cooler."

She smiled and nodded and off he went, Rayna at his heels.

As soon as he was gone, she felt bizarrely lonely, which annoyed her no end. She reminded herself for the umpteenth time that she was grateful to be here instead of staying at her parents' house until her condo was livable again. Hayes had no responsibility to hang out in the house keeping her company. In fact, it was better that he didn't, given that she had way too much of a tendency to fall back into old patterns when he was around. What they'd shared was years ago and they were never going there again.

As soon as he was out the door, she put the leftover spaghetti and garlic bread away for tomorrow night, cleaned up the kitchen, ran a bunch of clothes through the washer and dryer, and tidied up the house a bit.

The next day, Hayes's high school buddies were back again. Before she headed to the inn, they ate breakfast and went out with Hayes to work. That night, Austin and Jake stayed for dinner, which worked out great because there was plenty of spaghetti left for everyone.

Plus, Hayes's buddies kept the conversation going, which made the meal a lot more pleasant than the night before.

On Tuesday at work, Chrissy got a call from her mom.

"Sweetie, you mentioned the other day that you would come for dinner soon. How about tonight? I'm making your favorite creamy herb pork chops."

Chrissy longed to say she just couldn't make it. She knew the topic for the evening would be something along the lines of what *could* she be thinking, to be bedding down at the End of the Road Ranch?

But why put off the inevitable? She'd promised to come for dinner soon, and she might as well get it over with. Plus, there were the pork chops cooked the way only her mom knew how. Her mouth watered just thinking about them.

When she called Hayes to back out on cooking for the boys that night, he said it was no problem. "The guys aren't staying for dinner. And I really need to drive over to Bronco and pay my dad a visit."

She stifled a laugh—but didn't hide it completely.

He grumbled, "What? You think that's funny? You know I don't get along with my dad."

"I do know, yeah. And that's why I laughed, because you sounded as eager to go visit Lionel as I am to spend my evening listening to my mother lecture me on my unfortunate life choices."

"What unfortunate choices have you made lately?" He sounded way too amused—and curious, too. Plus, they were having an actual conversation again, which was definite progress after the radio silence of the past two nights.

However, no way she was admitting outright that staying at the ranch was her bad choice *du jour* from her mom's point of view. "Got an hour? Because my mom has a whole bunch of my bad choices to discuss with me."

"Oh, I'll bet."

"See you tomorrow morning for breakfast," she said. "Drive carefully, Hayes."

"I will." And then he was gone.

And she ended up standing there in the inn's kitchen, holding her phone, smiling because she and Hayes had just exchanged a few friendly words.

That evening, the pork chops were every bit as good as Chrissy had known they would be. And her mom ran true to form.

As Chrissy savored her first yummy bite of the delicious creamy dish, Patrice started in on her. "Honestly, sweetheart. You should be here with us until the issues at your condo are resolved. I was thinking that after dinner, we could caravan out to the Parker place—you, your dad and me. I'm sure whatever things you have at the ranch house will fit into three vehicles. It'll be quick and simple and from tonight on, you're here with us, all comfy in your old room, until your place is ready for your return."

Chrissy enjoyed another bite of tender breaded pan-fried pork chop slathered in scrumptious sauce. "Mom. You've outdone yourself. This is so good."

"Thank you, sweetheart. What do you think?"

"Delicious. Absolutely delicious."

"Chrissy. You know very well I wasn't asking about the pork chops."

"Oh. Right. You mean your suggestion that I stay here instead of out at the ranch."

"Yes. What do you say?"

Chrissy slid a glance at her dad. Mel Hastings gave her a tender smile and then forked up a bite-sized wedge of beautifully browned oven-roasted baby potato. But as for coming to her rescue in the discussion with her mom, not a chance.

"Thanks so much, Mom," Chrissy said. "But I'm all settled in at the ranch."

Her mom frowned. "But should you be taking advantage of the Parkers that way?"

Chrissy tamped down a spike of irritation. Her mom had a way of pushing all her buttons. "There's nobody there, Mom. Hayes's brothers aren't at home right now. Rylee's engaged and moved out for good. It's just Hayes and me staying there—and I'm pitching in, doing my part, cooking and helping around the house while Norma is spending most of her time over at Bronco Valley Hospital with Lionel."

Her mother said just what Chrissy should have known she would say. "Hmm. Just you and Hayes. Is that wise?"

Shaking her head, Chrissy drew a slow, calming breath. "Don't, Mom. Just don't."

"You're right," her mom said sweetly. "You're an adult and your life is your own."

"Thank you for acknowledging that."

"And as for your helping out at the Parker place, of course you are. You've always been helpful, always happy to do your share. But the ranch is out of town. It's a longer drive to work for you, whereas we're right here, a few blocks from your job."

It went on like that for the rest of the meal, her mom coming up with new reasons why Chrissy would be better off moving back home for now, and Chrissy insisting that she intended to remain at the ranch.

At a little after eight when she finally left, she was promising herself she would avoid having dinner at her mom's until she was back in her condo again. From now on, even creamy herb pork chops wouldn't tempt her to change her mind.

* * *

Hayes was sitting on the sofa staring blindly at the front door across the room when he heard a vehicle drive up outside.

At his feet, Rayna stirred. "Stay." He patted her head, and she settled back down.

A car door slammed. A minute later, he heard light footsteps on the porch. The front door opened.

"Hey." It was Chrissy in her work skirt and vest, with a stressed expression on her face.

"Hi," he replied without much enthusiasm.

Her low, chunky heels tapped the hardwood floor as she came closer. Setting her small shoulder bag on the big pine coffee table, she dropped into a chair across from him. "How's your dad doing?"

Rayna sat up and gave a questioning whine.

"Go ahead," he said to the dog. She went to Chrissy, who scratched her around the ruff and told her what a good dog she was.

Chrissy glanced up from petting his dog. "Hayes."

"Huh?"

"Your dad?"

He shook his head. "What can I say? He never changes. He hates being in the hospital. He's worried about the money it's costing for him to be there. The stress isn't good for him, and his bad attitude will probably keep him there longer—and anything I say flat out pisses him off. I drove all the way to Bronco and back and for what? Apparently, to listen to him complain about every little thing and remind me of all the things that need doing here, as if I didn't know."

"It's good that you went."

"I'm glad somebody thinks so."

Her eyes were softer than ever and full of understanding. "He's a good guy, your dad."

"I keep trying to remember that. But it's been so damn long since I saw his good side, it's way too easy to forget that he has one."

"Your dad was always friendly and sweet to me," she said with a tiny smile.

"He always liked you a hell of a lot better than he ever did me."

"Oh, come on. That's not true."

"Right. And enough about my dad." He leaned in and braced his forearms on spread knees. "How was dinner with the folks?"

She wrinkled her nose at him. "You had to ask."

"Sorry." He winked at her.

She scoffed. "No, you're not. As for how it went at my mom's, I'm looking on the bright side."

"Which is?"

"I got through it."

"So how *is* your mom?"

"Smart-ass," she muttered as she grabbed one of his mom's hand-hooked throw pillows off the end of the sofa and threw it at him.

Laughing for the first time since he left for Bronco that afternoon, he caught the pillow and tucked it under his arm. "What?" He pretended to look surprised. "Don't tell me you've got a problem with your mom."

"Ha. As if you didn't know. However, as I just said, I got through it. And by that I mean all the way through dinner and dessert. I even hung around afterward to listen to more of her unsolicited advice."

"Fun, huh?"

"That's probably not the word I would use. At least she didn't bring up Sam again, so that's a plus."

Hayes really wanted to ask her what had happened, exactly, with her ex. But how many times did he have to remind himself that he needed to keep things casual with her, not to delve too deeply into her past or her private life? They shared a slightly shaky friendship now and that was how it was supposed to stay. Which meant he needed to keep all his personal questions about her life and her marriage to himself.

She went on. "Anyway, I had dinner at my folks' house and it's over and I got through it without saying anything I wish I hadn't."

"Sounds like a win to me."

"Yeah. Right. A win. That's what I'm calling it, too." She grabbed her purse and rose. "Okay, so I've got a couple of menus to tweak before I can finalize what I need to order for next week's events. See you in the morning?"

"You bet."

She went up the stairs. He flopped back in the chair and stared at the rough beams overhead and tried not to wish she'd hung around to talk with him a little longer.

Yeah, he and Chrissy were supposed to be keeping their distance from each other and he was trying his hardest to do that. But it didn't escape his notice that the only time he'd felt good about anything today was the past few minutes he'd spent with her.

The next morning, none of his buddies could get away to help out. After Hayes took care of early chores and chowed down on the excellent breakfast Chrissy prepared for the two of them, she headed off to work and he decided it was time to face the End of the Road Ranch's financial reality.

In the cramped office at the back of the house he booted up the ancient PC, typed in the password that hadn't changed since he left home and opened the accounting software.

The news was pretty much what he'd expected—not good. And the stack of overdue bills waiting on one corner of his dad's rollback desk needed attention ASAP.

The ranch had come down to Lionel from Hayes's grandparents, so at least they owned the land, the house, the stock and the outbuildings. But they were definitely in arrears.

He'd been sitting at the computer, getting a handle on the grave situation for three hours when his mom spoke from the open doorway behind him. "Here you are…"

He turned around in the old oak swivel chair. Norma stood there, arms crossed, leaning against the door frame. "Hey, Mom. What's up? Need some help?"

"No. But thank you. I'm going to unpack the groceries I brought and do a little cooking. I can easily handle that myself." She pressed her lips together. "Going over the books, huh?"

He nodded. "We should talk, Mom."

She let her arms drop to her sides. "Yes. All right. I'll just put the perishables away and make some coffee."

Twenty minutes later, she set a full mug on the coaster by the old computer. "Here you go."

"Thanks." He took a sip.

She rolled the other chair over, sat beside him and put her hand on his arm. "You look as discouraged as I feel right now."

"Well, the numbers don't lie and the truth they're telling is not a happy truth."

"Honestly, we were breaking even until the past couple of months. Barely. But still. We were scraping by even after

Miles left for the service. But your father was so worried. And when he gets worried, he gets—"

"Bossy and mean."

Her eyes were so sad. "That's not what I was going to say."

"But I don't hear you denying it."

"Yeah, well…" Her voice trailed off. Finally she added, "He's too old to be so frustrated all the time."

"You're right. It's making him sick."

She nodded. "Last night, when it was just the two of us in that hospital room, he admitted that he's got to get a handle on his attitude and his temper. He says he's trying, and he plans to try harder."

There were any number of snarky remarks Hayes might have made right then, but he kept his mouth firmly shut.

His mom said, "Your dad was extra hard on Braden after Miles left."

"It's what Dad does. You'd think at some point he'd start to realize that he's the one with the problem."

"He does realize, and he just feels terrible."

"Right."

"After Miles left, your dad and Braden were arguing constantly. At first, they would patch it up and move on. But the tension just escalated."

"Until Braden couldn't take it anymore."

A small, sad sound escaped her. "That's about the size of it. So then Braden took off and your dad and I, we tried to keep things going. Too bad we're not getting any younger. We should have hired a hand, but—"

"There was no money to pay wages."

"That's right. It's a vicious circle."

Leaning her way, he wrapped an arm across her shoulders. "And on the subject of wages, Jake, Austin and Beck have done more than enough to help out around here. They can't keep showing up, working for free. They've got lives and jobs of their own."

"I know. And I am so grateful for all they've done around here."

"I know you are and so do they. And now, I need to hire at least one capable, hardworking cowhand to keep this place running. With me and a good hand putting in full days, we could manage for now."

"We don't have the—"

"Money. I know. So don't worry about it. I have some money put aside. I'll pay the new hire."

She gasped. "Oh, Hayes. We can't ask that of you."

"You're not asking. I'm just saying I'm hiring a hand, and it will be on my own dime."

"You know your father is going to order you not to."

Hayes gave a low chuckle at that. "He's not really in a position to stop me right now. If he wants to make the decisions around here again, he should put all his effort into getting well."

She was silent. He figured she was marshalling more arguments against him spending his money to keep the ranch afloat.

But then she said, "He never did disinherit you, you know."

That shocked him. "The day I left, he swore that he would."

"He lied. He would never do that to any of you kids. But he didn't want you to go, he lost his temper, and he let his big mouth write a check his heart was never going to let him cash."

"Well." Warmth stole through him. His dad could be a pigheaded ass. But he did have a heart and an ingrained sense of what was right. "Okay then, Mom. When Dad's pride gets the best of him because I'm paying the new hand, I'll just tell him that I'm protecting my interest in the End of the Road Ranch."

"That conversation probably won't go well."

"Too bad. I'm doing it, so one way or another, he's going to have to deal." Hayes picked up the stack of bills. "And now we need to talk about paying what's due."

She snatched the stack from him. "I'll pay those."

He gaped at her. "With what?"

"My freedom money."

He puzzled over that for a minute before shrugging and asking, "What is freedom money?"

A sly smile twisted her mouth. "When your Grandma Tessa passed, she left me a nice chunk of change. She knew I would never leave your father, but she believed a woman should have money of her own, freedom money, so she would always have an option if things got bad or she wanted to treat herself to a little getaway. I put my freedom money away for the time when I really needed it."

"Does Dad know about this freedom money of yours?"

"Of course. He would never touch it, and he's not going to be happy I'm spending it on a stack of bills. I've tried more than once in the past month to convince him we need to use my money to help save the ranch. He said no, absolutely not. And up until today, I have backed down. But, honey, you have inspired me."

"What?" He wasn't following. "How?"

"The way I see it, if you can use your money to get us the help we need around here, I can use mine to pay bills. I love your father with all my heart. But Lionel does not get to decide what makes me free. I decide that. And having at least some of the bills paid—that's freedom to me."

For a moment, her eyes sparkled, and her smile was the

bright, happy smile he remembered from way back when he was seven or eight, before things started to get tough at the End of the Road Ranch. But then, much too soon, the look of joy faded from his mother's face.

"Mom." He put his arm around her again. "What's wrong?"

She leaned against him. "The truth is, my freedom money isn't going to go all that far."

"We'll make it work."

She touched his cheek, a fond brush of her fingers against his skin. "Oh, honey. I'm so glad you're here—and I hope we can find our way through this rough patch. But sometimes it feels like all we've had the past twenty years are rough patches."

"We will make it through," he said, shocking himself with how confident he sounded.

"I do hope you're right. I hope we can hold on, stick with it until we come out stronger on the other side. After all, they don't call this town Tenacity for nothing."

He scoffed. "No. They call it Tenacity because some early settler had a dark sense of humor."

His mom shook her head slowly, a faraway look in her eyes. "We *are* tenacious—tenacious and all those words that mean the same thing. We are stubborn. Obstinate. Determined. I mean, look at your father. Things just keep going from bad to worse and still, he swears he'll never give up, never sell."

"Because he won't, Mom."

"I know, I know. But, Hayes, to tell you the truth, lately it just feels like it's only a matter of time before we have no choice. And now there's the cost of Lionel's medical care on top of everything else."

"But you have insurance." He'd seen her hand over her

insurance card that first day, when they rushed his dad to the hospital.

"Yes, we have insurance, and so far we've managed to keep up with the payments, but the insurance is not going to cover everything. Plus, well…" She glanced away.

"Just say it, Mom."

"All right. Your father *is* getting better. He's lost a little weight, and he will be losing some more with the diet he's on that he's promised to stick to when he's finally back home. But he's not getting better fast enough. It's been five days since the surgery and the doctor won't release him. Not for a while, the doctor says."

"What are you telling me? Is Dad okay?"

"Yes—or he will be, I'm sure. The doctor says so. But it's taking him longer than anticipated to be ready to come home."

"Mom. Just don't worry. He's going to be all right. And I will keep things going here. We won't give up. We'll make it through."

Hayes kind of marveled at the words coming out of his own mouth. After so many years of swearing he wanted nothing to do with the End of the Road Ranch, now he was seeing the truth he'd started facing two months ago when Braden called out of the blue to say Miles was gone and he was leaving.

The plain truth was, when Hayes had walked away, he'd never once doubted that his family would keep the ranch going. He'd sworn never to come back, and he hadn't. Not for fifteen years.

But for all that time, he'd had the sure and certain knowledge that home was there, that it always would be. That his mom and dad would grow old on the ranch, that his brothers and his sister would always be around to help out when needed. Together they would overcome any obstacle no matter what fate threw at them.

Well, there had been a lot of obstacles. Too many, as it turned out. His brothers had filled him in on all the challenges as the years went by.

Fate had not been kind to the Parker family. There had been years of drought followed by years of blizzards that tore across the land and froze the cattle where they stood. His dad had needed to change things, to be more flexible in order to stay in the black, but Lionel Parker had never been real big on change.

And now, it had gotten bad enough for his family that losing the ranch seemed inevitable to his mom.

"I'm sorry," his mom whispered. "I shouldn't be so negative."

He drew her close yet again. "It's going to be okay, Mom. We'll see it through."

"Oh, I do hope you're right."

"Count on it."

"You're a good son," she whispered. "I'm grateful for you, Hayes. So grateful for all four of you kids."

He hugged her closer as she sagged against him.

But Norma Parker was no quitter. Seconds later, she drew herself up. "Alrighty, then. Enough of this feeling sorry for myself. I've got lots to do and I may as well stop whining and get after it." She stood. "I noticed Chrissy's been cooking. There's a pot roast in the slow cooker. Smells good."

"Yeah, it does."

His mom scolded, "She works all day and also cooks for you."

"She insisted she had to help out or she couldn't stay here."

"I know, honey. She told me that, too. I'm going to pitch in a little on the cooking front."

"You know you'll just piss Chrissy off if you do that."

His mom grinned. "She's a spunky one, that girl." The stack of bills in her hand, Norma pushed her chair back where it belonged and left the small room.

Hayes shut down the old PC and then just sat there for a bit, staring at the dark screen, realizing all over again that, for him, there was no making peace with losing the ranch. He would do whatever he had to do. One way or another, he would see to it that the ranch remained in the family's hands.

Chapter Five

Chrissy left the inn at a little after four that day. She stopped by her condo, where the workmen were ripping out ruined sheetrock. It looked like a disaster zone. She didn't stay long.

At the ranch, Hayes was apparently out somewhere on the land. She ran upstairs and changed into jeans and a T-shirt.

When she came back down, she discovered that Norma had been there. And she'd been cooking. A foil-covered squash casserole waited in the fridge, along with Swiss steak in a red-topped Tupperware container. There was mac and cheese, too. Chrissy shook her head at the sight of all that food. She wouldn't have to cook for a few days at least, that was for sure.

And tonight, the roast she'd put in the slow cooker before she left for work that morning was ready to go. All she really had to do to get dinner on was set the table for two, toss a salad and plate the food.

Hayes came in at five thirty and headed straight for a shower. She had the food on the table when he came back down. He seemed bothered, somehow. Preoccupied. The meal was mostly silent.

Afterward, he disappeared into the office in back, Rayna at his heels. Chrissy straightened up the kitchen and then headed for the mudroom where she'd left a pair of sturdy old shoes. She put them on, grabbed Norma's gardening gloves and went out to the garden where the early evening shadows had pushed back the heat of the afternoon.

For an hour, she pulled weeds and picked green beans, peppers and broccoli. By then, it was getting dark. She went inside, took off her dirty shoes and Norma's gloves, and left them in the mudroom. Barefoot, she carried the basket of vegetables to the laundry room and washed them in the sink there.

The house seemed so quiet. She checked the office. Empty. Had Hayes gone up to his room already?

She considered going on up herself. Instead, she wandered into the great room and then out the front door.

Hayes was sitting on the porch steps, Rayna stretched out behind him. She stepped over the big dog and plunked down at his side.

"Your mom's been cooking," she accused. "Tell her I said to stop that."

He shot her a glance and then went back to staring out into the gathering darkness. Somewhere out there, a nighthawk let out its short, strangled cry. "I already told her you had the cooking under control."

"Well, she didn't listen."

"Sorry. Best I could do."

Bracing an elbow on her knee, Chrissy rested her chin on the heel of her hand. "So…what's up?"

Several seconds went by before he answered. "It's nothing too terrible. My dad's going to be in the hospital for a while longer."

"You're worried about him."

"Yeah. A little. My mom says he'll be all right, but he's

not improving as fast as they'd hoped—and I'm also kind
of down about the ranch's financial situation."

"Is it bad?"

"Bad enough." He turned his head her way. Their gazes
locked. "Today I called a friend I met in Washington state.
We worked together on the ranch that my wife's dad, Jacob
Grantham, used to own. My friend, Arlen Hawk, will be
here tomorrow or maybe Friday. I can use a good hand and
Arlen's the best."

"Makes sense. I'll clear my stuff out of Braden's room
tomorrow for him."

"No need. Arlen's got a fancy rig—a one-ton Chevy Sil-
verado pickup pulling a combo trailer."

"He brings his living quarters *and* his horse?"

"That's right."

"Sounds like a good friend to have."

"He is. You'll like him."

"I have no doubt." She was still thinking about what he'd
said a minute before. "You mentioned that your wife's dad
used to own the ranch where you met her?"

"Yeah." He stared off to the west as the last rays of day-
light slipped behind the low humps of the distant hills.

Just when she thought he'd said all he intended to say,
he turned to her again. His eyes were full of shadows. She
had no idea what he might be thinking, though she guessed
he was about to say that he didn't want to talk about his
dead wife's dad, and she ought to mind her own business.

But he surprised her. "My wife, Anna, was Jacob's only
child. Anna's mom had died when Anna was a little girl.
Jacob raised her on his own and Anna was everything to
him. When she died, it broke him. He just didn't have the
heart to go on running the family ranch. He turned the

place over to his younger brothers and retired. A year later, he died of a stroke."

She hardly knew what to say. "Hayes. I'm so sorry…"

"Me, too." He looked down at his boots. "Jacob was a good guy. The best. But the truth is, I think he was ready to go."

"And… Anna?"

He made a low, thoughtful sound—and fell silent. She accepted the fact that he wasn't going to answer the question she hadn't had the courage to ask clearly.

But then he said, "Car accident. Black ice. The Grantham Ranch is in eastern Washington. Anna was on her way home from Christmas shopping in Seattle. She hit that patch of ice and ended up wrapped around a Douglas fir tree. Died instantly, they said. People said that was a blessing. I don't know, though. Nothing about Anna's death feels like a blessing to me."

"Oh, Hayes…" She shouldn't touch him. She knew that. But she took his hand anyway and eased her fingers between his warm, rough ones. He didn't pull back, so she turned her body toward him. "I don't know what to say, except how sorry I am that you lost her."

"Thanks." He stared into the middle distance. "Anna was a happy person. Nothing got her down. It was hell losing her, but I'm grateful for the five years we had together."

Out in the dark, another night bird let out a lonely trill of sound.

Hayes said, "And now that we're sitting here talking about all the tough things…"

"Go ahead. I'm listening."

"My mom thinks it's just a matter of time until we have to sell the ranch."

"Oh, no."

"Well, it's definitely a possibility."

"You're saying that you think she's right?"

He didn't answer her question. Instead, he said, "All these years, I've told myself I didn't care about this place."

She whispered, "But you do."

"Yeah. Now that losing the ranch is a real possibility, I just can't stand for that to happen."

"So then, don't *let* it happen."

He laughed, a rueful sound. "Easy-peasy, huh?"

"Hey. If anyone can save this place, it's you, Hayes."

"Is this a pep talk?"

"Absolutely."

Behind them, Rayna stretched, yawned, and settled back down again with a long sigh.

Leaning sideways, Hayes bumped Chrissy's shoulder with his. "Your turn."

She faked a wide-eyed glance. "My turn for what?"

"I told you about Anna. Now, you tell me about Sam Shaw."

She let go of his hand and pretended to scowl at him. "I'm not sure I like where this is going, mister."

"Too bad. Talk."

She thought of how good Hayes had been to her, coming to her rescue last Friday night at the bar, moving her in here so she wouldn't have to live at her mom's again. Yeah, they were trying to straddle a tough line, be friendly but not *too* friendly.

But where was that line, exactly?

Right now, she wasn't even sure she cared. If he wanted to hear about Sam, she would tell him. "Sam is nothing like you."

He smirked at her. "Should I be insulted?"

"Please don't. What I mean is, Sam's a by-the-book kind of person. Or he was when I met him. He was one of those guys who had created a solid career that provided a good living so that he could get married and have kids. He defined himself by that, by his role as the man of the family. He is—or he *was*—a truly traditional kind of guy."

"And you liked that?"

"I liked that he was a family man at heart, that he wanted all the time-honored things, a good marriage and kids to see through to adulthood. I'd finished college and I had a job I loved. I was ready to get married at that point. But then, as soon as we got back from the honeymoon, he began pushing me to quit work and start having babies."

"But wasn't that what you wanted?"

"I did, yes, but not immediately. I wanted a little time just for the two of us. But he was so insistent. In the end, we agreed we would start trying right away, and I would keep my job until I got pregnant."

"And…?"

"Three years went by, and I never got pregnant. We finally went to a specialist about the problem and found out that we were not going to be having a biological child together."

Hayes studied her face. She waited for him to ask her outright if she was infertile.

But he surprised her. He let it be. Let her say what she was willing to say, tell the story in her own way.

She went on, "Sam couldn't deal with not being able to have a baby with me. He had this idea of what a family should be. A dad and a mom and children they made together. If it couldn't be that way, he wasn't interested."

"Whoa." Hayes said the word in a sympathetic whisper.

"I don't think he even imagined our marriage would be any other way than how he planned it. Not until the worst happened and he realized he wasn't going to get the life he'd always wanted. It threw him. He had no backup plan."

"So…just like that, you broke up?"

She considered how much to share. Despite the disaster that her marriage became, she still felt a certain obligation to her ex-husband. She still had sympathy for him. Sam always had such conviction about how things should be. And when he'd suddenly found out life wasn't going to turn out as he believed it should, he just didn't know where to go from there.

"We didn't break up immediately. But things went from bad to worse. Sam spiraled into a depression. He started drinking. He was uncommunicative. He wouldn't even consider counseling, wouldn't put any effort into finding workable solutions to our problems. Two years after we went to that specialist together, Sam announced that he wanted a divorce."

Now Hayes was the one taking her hand, weaving their fingers together.

She gave him a misty smile. "By then, I was pretty much at my wit's end with him. I asked him—again—to go to counseling. He said no. He said that our marriage was over. There was no point, he said, in pretending there was anything left to save."

"Wow. Talk about cold."

"But see, by then, I agreed with him. I was ready to move on."

"So then, that was it for the two of you?"

"Yeah. That was it. We divided our assets down the middle and split up. Sam moved to Florida, bought a boat and set out to…find himself, I guess you could say. I moved back home and started over."

Hayes put his arm around her. She allowed herself to

lean on him. "You're strong and smart and tough, too," he said. "You can do just about anything you set your mind to. You're going to be fine, Chrissy Hastings. You know that, right?"

She chuckled. "Going to be? Hayes Parker, I *am* fine."

"You certainly are," he agreed with a grin.

She grinned right back at him. "Why, thank you."

"Don't thank me. It's only the truth." His eyes gleamed jade green. And his lips were so close...

Uh-uh, she reminded herself. *Not going to happen.*

Gently, she pulled away from him. "I should go in."

His grin was gone now. "Got it. Night, Chrissy."

She rose. "Night, Hayes." She was careful not to glance back at him as she crossed the porch and went inside.

Hayes *had* wanted to kiss her. He'd wanted that a lot.

But she'd stopped it.

And he respected her decision.

He was careful the next morning to be no more than casually friendly. She seemed to accept that he'd gotten her message. They were back on an even keel with each other.

That evening, the two of them had just sat down to eat when Hayes heard a truck pull in out front. "I'm thinking that might be Arlen," he said, sliding his napkin in by his plate and pushing back his chair. "Excuse me."

She nodded. "I'll set another place."

"Great. It'll be a few minutes. He'll need to put his horse in the pasture out behind the barn."

Arlen was coming up the front steps when Hayes opened the door. Tall and broad with mahogany skin and startling blue eyes, Arlen spread both long arms wide and kept coming. "Hayes Parker. It's been way too long."

The men met on the porch for a hug and some back-slapping. When they pulled apart, Hayes said, "Swiss steak tonight. You had dinner yet?"

His friend shook his head. "Not yet—and Swiss steak sounds grand."

"You got it. Let me show you where to take your horse and park your trailer, then we can eat."

Fifteen minutes later, Arlen's horse was free in the horse pasture, and his truck and trailer were parked just beyond the backyard gate. He had his own generator and Hayes had shown him the outside faucet so he could hook up his hose for water. They returned to the house, where they washed up in the mudroom and then joined Chrissy at the kitchen table.

Hayes thought his friend and Chrissy hit it off nicely. Chrissy laughed at Arlen's funny stories of his years working on ranches from Southern California to the wilds of New Jersey.

Later, Hayes followed Arlen out back for a drink. In the trailer's small kitchen, they sat at the table. Arlen poured them each two fingers of the good stuff and then raised his glass. "To you, back home at last." They drank and set their glasses down. "Kind of proves that old adage, *never say never.*"

Hayes moved his empty shot glass in a slow circle on the tabletop. "You're right. I always vowed I would never come back to this town."

"And yet here you are." They laughed together at that. And then Arlen said, "And not only did you come back, but you also have the one and only Chrissy Hastings living with you in your house."

Arlen was a few years older. Hayes used to confide in him, especially at first, before Hayes and Anna got close.

Hayes pushed his glass across the table. "Since you're saving my sorry ass here, I'm just going to let you yank my chain all you want."

Arlen refilled both their glasses. "I believe you once said that Chrissy Hastings ripped your heart out and put it through a shredder, that you would never let a woman get hold of your heart again."

"I was young. Young with a tendency toward embarrassing exaggerations."

"And yet, you found happiness with Anna—bless her sweet soul."

"To Anna—and Jacob." Hayes offered the toast. They both drank, after which they shared a moment of silence in honor of Hayes's lost wife and her big-hearted dad.

After such a solemn toast, Hayes dared to hope Arlen was done busting his balls.

No such luck. "And now you've got Chrissy sleeping in the same house with you, serving up the Swiss steak with that fine, glowing smile."

"We're friends now, Chrissy and me. That's all, nothing more."

Arlen folded his muscled forearms on the table and leaned across to grin at Hayes. "You're a goner for that girl, my friend. You might as well face it."

Hayes shot his friend a narrow-eyed glare. "I'm so happy to be a source of amusement for you."

"Go ahead. Blow me off. I can take it."

"Friends, Arlen. Chrissy and I are friends."

"Keep saying that, my friend. But the truth is the truth and in the end, a man can't hide from it."

The next morning before dawn when Hayes took Rayna out to tackle early chores, Arlen was waiting on the back porch. The men headed for the barn, the dog trotting at their heels.

Two hours later, Chrissy served them breakfast. They

went back to work with full bellies and spent the day switching out mineral barrels, moving cattle and chasing down strays.

They were back at the house by five, going their separate ways to clean up. Chrissy served dinner at six. At a little after seven, Arlen retired to the trailer.

Through the window above the sink, Chrissy watched him go. "I like him." She loaded water glasses into the dishwasher.

Hayes rinsed the last plate and handed it over. "Yeah. Arlen's the real deal. Whatever needs doing, he's right on top of it. He knows horses and cattle. And he's always got a friend's back. He's the best. I'm hoping we can mostly keep a handle on all the work around here, just him and me. Which is saying something, let me tell you."

She loaded in that last plate, shut the dishwasher and started it up, then grabbed the hand towel and wiped her hands dry. "I'm glad you have help."

Damn. She really was way too pretty and always had been, with that sleek and shining coffee-colored hair, and those eyes that made a man feel like he could fall right into them.

"Hayes?"

He blinked. "What?"

"Nothing." She laughed. The sound curled down around inside him, warm and so sweet. "Seemed like you drifted away there for a minute."

Arlen was right, he though grimly. *I'm in big trouble with this woman. In big trouble all over again.*

He knew he should avoid her, say he had the accounts to go over in the office, or just say good-night and head up to his room, maybe read a damn book. He opened his mouth to say he had...things to do.

What he actually said was, "Want to sit out on the porch for a little while?"

Her smile was slow and sweet as honey—and maybe a little more than friends-only. "Sure."

They sat on the steps with Rayna sprawled out behind them and watched the colors of the sky change from orange and purple to darkest blue, the stars twinkling brighter as each minute passed. She said her day had been hectic, but she'd managed to stay on top of things.

When he asked how the work at her condo was going, she shrugged. "As well as can be expected, I guess."

"You know, you don't sound all that happy about the progress at your place."

"Yeah, well. My dad says these things take time. And I know he's right. But I'm impatient."

"It's understandable."

She shot him a wary look. "Hayes, I have to ask you…" Her voice trailed off.

"Whatever it is, just say it."

"Okay. Am I wearing out my welcome here?"

He blinked in surprise. "Hell, no. Are you kidding? Don't tell me you're thinking of leaving now."

"No, I just…" Her gaze slid away.

"You just, what?"

"Well, I don't want to take advantage of you, that's all."

"Take advantage? You're not." He touched her knee. When she finally looked at him, he said, "Please. You are not in any way taking advantage. You work nonstop around here after working all day at the inn." He took her hand. Maybe he shouldn't. Maybe that was once again stepping over that invisible line between friendship and something more.

Well, too damn bad. She needed a place until her condo

was livable again and there was no reason that place shouldn't be right here.

Chewing the inside of her lip, she gazed at him, wide-eyed, adorable in her uncertainty. "You really are sure about this?"

"You'd better believe it. It's working for me. When you go, my mom's going to insist on taking over, filling your shoes around here. Believe me she's got plenty going on trying to deal with my dad." Right then, it occurred to him that maybe being here wasn't working out for her, so he made himself address that. "Tell me the truth. Does it work for *you*, staying here?"

"Yes. Of course. It does. It's just…" She eased her hand from his grip.

He studied her face. "Wait a minute. Did something happen today?"

She groaned then and tipped her head up to the sky. "On the way back here after work, I stopped in to check on the work at the condo. My mom was there. 'Just wanted to see how things are going,' she said in her sweetest voice. And then she started in on me again, that I was taking advantage of you, that I needed to come back home and stay with her and Dad because that's where I belong at a time like this."

"The question is do you *want* to go stay with your folks?"

She laughed. There was no humor in the sound. "Dear God in heaven, no!"

"Then what are we talking about? You're staying, and I'm damn grateful that you are." He took her hand again.

She didn't pull away that time—in fact, she held on. "Well, then. Okay. I'll stay."

"Whew. You had me scared for a minute there…" The sentence kind of trailed off. He realized he was staring at her mouth, remembering what it felt like, kissing her, holding her soft, curvy body in his arms. "I, uh…"

"Hmm?"

"Um. Good. Just… It's good that you're staying. Thank you. For staying."

She let out another trill of laughter. "Okay. You can stop now. You've definitely convinced me."

He grinned. "Finally."

"But still, I was thinking…"

Now what? "Yeah?"

"Well, I was wondering…" She seemed flustered, her cheeks pink, her eyes overly bright.

"Go ahead," he coaxed. "Hit me with it."

"Well, I was wondering if maybe you were free tomorrow night? I was thinking we could go to Castillo's, my treat." The small Mexican restaurant was a block down from the Grizzly, on the opposite side of the street. "I'll just come back here after I'm done at the inn. I can change out of my work clothes and then we can drive into town together."

Faintly, way in the back of his mind, alarm bells were going off. Wouldn't that be too much like a date?

Chrissy was still talking. "I mean, you know, completely casual—meaning, as friends. It's not much, just a dinner out. But I could really use a change of pace, to do something a little different, you know? And more than that, it's a way I can show my appreciation to you for giving me a place to stay."

We shouldn't. It's a bad idea. She really wants to keep it friends-only. And that place has dangerous memories. They used to eat at Castillo's, the two of them, back when they were a couple. The food was really good, and the prices were reasonable. It was the perfect date-night spot for a pair of high school kids.

So what? he reminded himself. *High school was a long time ago. This, now, is friends-only. Don't go making it a big deal when it's anything but.*

You're kidding yourself, he silently scoffed. *Look at you. Arlen's right. You're into her, you know you are. And look at her, with that soft smile, so hopeful and sweet. You know where this is going.*

To Castillo's, as friends. That's where.

Man. He was losing it, arguing with himself inside his own head.

It feels like more.

Well, it's not. So get over yourself and say yes.

No. It's a bad idea. He started to tell her that. But when he opened his mouth, he heard himself saying, "I would love to go to Castillo's with you tomorrow night."

"You would?" Her smile bloomed even bigger. That smile was everything. It reminded him that life was not only struggle, pain and disappointment. There was beauty, too. And good people, like Chrissy, good people just trying to do the right thing and get by day-to-day.

"Yeah," he said. "Come on back to the ranch after work and we'll ride into town together."

Chapter Six

Chrissy had always loved Castillo's. Growing up, her parents used to take her there. She would order a chicken burrito and savor every bite. The small restaurant was cozy and a little dark, a narrow storefront with two rows of wooden booths, and a small bar in back.

Pablo and Yolanda Castillo owned and ran the place. They were in their early sixties now. Yolanda served the food. Their older son tended the bar and their younger son helped Pablo in the kitchen.

That night, Yolanda greeted Chrissy and Hayes with a big smile and led them to a booth back near the bar. They asked for frosty, delicious margaritas and quesadillas to start. The carne asada was the best, so they both ordered that, too.

"I love it here," Chrissy said, feeling downright nostalgic as they sipped their drinks and devoured the quesadillas. "It's just so…homey."

"You're right." He took a bite of quesadilla. "So good. Remember the times we came here together?"

"Oh, yeah. We always had beef tacos and tall glasses of Dr Pepper."

"Yeah. I felt so grownup and manly, taking my girl out to eat…" His big smile faded. He set down the wedge of cheese-filled tortilla.

"What's wrong?"

"It's just that I've been thinking about what you said the other night, about your ex, about how he had an idea of the way things should be, how he couldn't cope when things didn't fit into his plans. And the more I think about it, the more wrong that seems to me. Because people ought to be able to work together, right? We should all try to roll with the punches when things get tough."

"I agree." She sipped her drink. "But Sam didn't seem to be able to do that."

"So he just walked away from you."

"In the end, yeah."

Hayes picked up his margarita and then set it back down without drinking from it. "I keep thinking about that. I keep thinking that I did pretty much the same damn thing to you. I said marry me now or it's over. And when you tried to explain that you weren't ready for marriage yet, I wouldn't listen. I said we were done, and I sent you away."

The regret on his face? It broke something open down inside her. She ached for him at the same time as she felt lighter, freer. Never in a hundred years would she have expected him to admit that he'd dumped her for not doing things his way. Even if it was the truth.

And he wasn't through. "I shouldn't have done that, Chrissy. Shouldn't have laid down that ultimatum, shouldn't have demanded that you marry me right then."

She wanted to reach across and lay her hand on his. But she held herself back. She'd taken his hand more than once last night and the other night, too. She had to stop doing that. Innocent touches could too easily lead to intimate ones. And they'd agreed they weren't going there. "Hayes. We were so young."

"Too young." He added, more softly, "Though I never would have admitted it then."

"You just…needed someone to be on your side, no matter what."

"I did. I needed someone willing to stand with me come hell or high water. I needed that so bad, Chrissy."

"And I couldn't be that for you then."

"Yeah. I get that now. You just weren't ready to leave everything behind for a mixed-up kid with no prospects."

"You're right," she answered honestly. "Except that it wasn't because you were kind of mixed up and not because you had no prospects, either. It was that I had things I needed to do, like get my degree, grow up a little. It wasn't about you, Hayes. I honestly wasn't ready to get married at that point. Not to you. Not to anyone."

"I should have waited. I should have had a little patience."

That made her smile. "It's so good to know that you can see my side of it now. But don't beat yourself up over it. You needed someone strong and sure to stand beside you then. I wasn't that person."

"I was so angry at you."

"I remember."

"And I've held on to that anger. When I first came back, when we ran into each other at the inn that first day, I still felt that way. I still saw you as having been the one in the wrong all those years ago. But tonight…"

"What? Tell me."

"Well, I'm starting to get that I was the unreasonable one."

"Now you're being too hard on yourself, Hayes."

"No. I'm just seeing the past in a different way, a more *real* way, that's all." He reached across the table and put his hand over hers.

She let him, though she knew she shouldn't.

A moment later, Yolanda appeared with the main course. Hayes pulled his hand away. They concentrated on the wonderful meal and left talk of the past behind.

When they got back to the ranch, Rayna was waiting just inside the front gate. They stopped to greet her, and she followed them up the steps.

"It's nice out tonight." Hayes paused on the porch and turned to stare up at the starry, cloudless sky. He glanced down and into Chrissy's eyes. "Another great night for sitting on the porch..."

She should probably go in. But she didn't have to work tomorrow. There was no big push to get to bed or anything.

They perched on the porch steps as they had those other nights, with Rayna flopping down, getting comfortable behind them.

"Thanks for dinner," he said.

"You're welcome. Castillo's never disappoints."

"You got that right."

She brought her knees up to the first step and rested her arms on them. He stared out at the sky as she studied his profile—the strong, straight nose, the sharp cheekbones and sculpted jawline.

When he turned his head her way, they ended up staring at each other. It was no hardship, staring at Hayes Parker. Never had been.

"What?" he asked, one corner of that too-sexy mouth quirking up.

"You tell me," she replied. It came out sounding like a challenge, though she hadn't meant it to be—or had she?

Hayes leaned closer. She didn't back away. Her heart

had set up a racket inside her chest. Her breath felt trapped in her lungs.

With some effort, she remembered to let the air out, to take in another breath.

Now everything felt slower, sweeter and a little bit magical.

The night around them seemed to hum and that hum was inside her, a yearning.

And a promise.

"I shouldn't," he said in a gruff whisper, his lips a breath's distance from hers now.

You're right. Don't. The words were there, trapped inside her mind, stilled by the hungry beating of her heart.

And then it happened. His mouth touched hers. A sound escaped her then, a sigh that got caught on a hint of a moan.

It was good. So good. After all these years. To feel his mouth on hers again.

At his gentle nudge, she parted her lips. His breath flowed into her.

It was so sweet, that kiss, full of tenderness and promise. It was all the good things they'd shared in the old days. It was the closeness, the soul-deep connection between them—the connection she'd severed by necessity so that she could get over him, get on with her life.

His hands clasped her shoulders. She sighed at his touch, expecting him to pull her closer.

Instead, very gently, he pushed her away.

She opened her eyes, stunned at what they'd just done. And even worse, at how much she'd wanted—still wanted—to keep right on doing it.

They stared at each other. He looked wrecked. She knew that she did, too.

"I'm sorry, Chrissy," he whispered, still holding her away from him. "I shouldn't have done that."

Her foolish heart cried, *Oh yes! Yes, you should have* at the same time as she knew very well that he was right. "Yeah," she said with a certainty she didn't feel. "I know. It's…not a good idea."

His grip on her shoulders loosened and his hands dropped away. "You okay?"

She tried on a smile as she lied outright. "I am. I'm fine." Forcing her wobbly legs to straighten, she rose to her feet. "I think I'll go in."

"All right, then. Thanks again for dinner."

"My pleasure." It was far too true. "Night."

"Good night." She stepped over Rayna and made for the door.

"What's going on with you and the ex-girlfriend?" Arlen asked the next morning after breakfast as they two of them mucked out the barn.

Hayes scooped up a shovelful of dirty straw. "No idea what you're talkin' about."

"Oh, really? You can't remember back as far as breakfast, with you and her being way too careful not to look at each other? And polite." Arlen let out a slow whistle. "Never seen manners like that so early in the morning."

"Let it go, Arlen."

That brought out Arlen's famous deep, knowing chuckle. "Never say I didn't warn you."

Hayes dumped the last shovelful of dirty straw on top of the pile in the wheelbarrow. "Pass me that broom, would you?"

Arlen handed it over and then clapped him on the shoulder. "You want to talk about it, you know I'm here for you, my friend."

Hayes longed to order the big cowhand to mind his own

damn business. But then he'd only end up feeling more like a jerk than he already did. "Thanks," he said through clenched teeth and started sweeping up straw.

All that day he felt bad. He'd been the one who started it with Chrissy, leaning in, taking that kiss that he couldn't stop thinking about. She'd kissed him back and it felt so good, her lips opening, welcoming.

Her kiss had worked a certain scary magic. It threw him back in time to all those years before, the two of them so in love they couldn't bear to be apart. Her mouth tasted like heaven. He'd wanted nothing so much as to haul her closer, kiss her more deeply, let the heat between them take control.

But they'd promised each other they weren't going to do that. So he'd stopped what he'd started—and yeah, he knew he'd hurt her feelings, running hot and then all of a sudden stopping things cold.

But it would be okay in a few days. The awkwardness between them would fade. They would get back to keeping it friendly, no pressure, no heat.

All he had to do was behave himself and the situation would work itself out. He could do that. No problem.

Except that later, at dinner, she remained so distant. So careful. He missed the new friendship they'd found.

And then, Monday morning, it was the same thing all over again. He left the breakfast table feeling like a stranger in the house where he'd grown up.

Chrissy was kind to him. She never once gave him a dirty look or raised her voice. But she was taking keeping distance between them very seriously. And by then, he'd started to wonder how long he could bear it, how soon he would break.

He just wanted their newfound friendship back, he kept telling himself. But then he would think about that kiss on the porch and a low, knowing voice in the back of his head would call him a liar for trying to tell himself that being just friends with Chrissy Hastings would ever be enough.

"There you are!" Chrissy turned at the sound of her friend Marisa's voice. Black-haired with beautiful brown eyes and lush curves, Marisa Sanchez stood in the open doorway of Chrissy's postage-stamp of an office at the Tenacity Inn.

"Hey, there! Right on time for lunch." Chrissy jumped up from her desk. Three steps later, she was hugging her friend.

Like Chrissy, Marisa had grown up in Tenacity. Marisa was younger, just twenty-six. But in Tenacity, everyone knew everyone, so they had always known each other, though they hadn't grown close until Chrissy returned to town after she and Sam broke up.

"This way." Chrissy took Marisa's hand and led her to the inn's dining room, where a light breakfast was served daily in addition to meals and snacks for events and the various mini conventions booked by local groups and businesses. She pulled out a chair at a two-top near a tall window looking out on a neatly landscaped section of the grounds. "Have a seat."

Marisa hesitated. "You know we could have gone to Castillo's or that little café next to the Grizzly."

The Silver Spur Café was mostly a breakfast place, but they served sandwiches, too. As for Castillo's? No, thank you. Not for a while. Right now, her favorite restaurant reminded her too sharply of Saturday night, of how absolutely great it had been.

Until it wasn't.

"Next time," Chrissy promised. Marisa took the offered

chair and Chrissy asked, "Cobb salad, iced tea and crusty bread with sweet butter?"

Marisa laughed. "Okay, that sounds perfect. Some other time for Castillo's."

"Sit right there. I'll be back in a flash." Chrissy had assembled the salads ahead of time and put the crusty loaf in the warming oven a few minutes before. She quickly served them both.

They settled in to catch up. Marisa was a fine musician who taught piano to quite a few people in town, kids and adults alike. She also had a real talent for organizing events. Nowadays, she was a local celebrity. Her video of the annual winter holiday choir right there in Tenacity had started out on TikTok and gone viral—as in all-the-way-around-the-globe viral. The choir's presentation was multicultural, funky and unique. Everyone in town had been thrilled that their small community had gained a moment in the spotlight.

"So what's new with you?" Chrissy asked.

Marisa set down her fork and clapped her hands together. "You won't believe it."

"What? Tell me!"

"You are looking at this year's director of the Mistletoe Christmas Pageant."

The Mistletoe Christmas Pageant took place in Bronco right along with the Mistletoe Rodeo, which was a very big deal. "Wow. Marisa. That's huge."

"I know! I can't believe they asked me. And I can still do our annual holiday show here in Tenacity, too."

"Right. Because the Mistletoe Christmas Pageant is in November and we do *our* Christmas show in December."

"You got it." Marisa beamed.

"This is fabulous!" Chrissy jumped up, ran around the

table, pulled her friend to her feet and hugged her good and hard—yeah, they were huggers, the two of them. She loved that about their friendship. "You are brilliant," she said. "And I'm so glad you're getting the recognition and the great projects you deserve."

"Thank you. Me, too." Marisa hugged her right back.

Chrissy returned to her seat.

As she smoothed her napkin over her lap, Marisa asked, "So how are the condo repairs going?"

"Much too slowly if you ask me." Last week, when Chrissy called Marisa to invite her to lunch, she'd brought her friend up to speed on the condo disaster. "As of now, my dad assures me that things are moving right along— but it's going to be another three or four weeks, and that's if I'm lucky. The whole interior had to be torn out to the studs. It's a major rebuild."

"But your insurance will cover it?"

"Yeah. Luckily I purchased really good coverage when I moved in. And now I'm so glad I did."

"Excellent."

They ate in silence for a minute or two. When Chrissy glanced up from her plate again, Marisa was grinning at her across the table. "Okay," Chrissy said. "What is going through that mind of yours? Tell me now."

"Hmm…" Marisa actually wiggled her eyebrows.

"What are you up to? Don't tease me. Put it out there, whatever it is."

"Well, I'm just wondering how it's going, you living at the End of the Road Ranch with Hayes."

Chrissy groaned. "What have you heard?"

"Well…" Marisa drew that one word out for way too long.

"Now you really are just teasing me. Spill it."

"Okay, fine. Rumor is, you were seen with him Saturday night at Castillo's."

"What? Two people can't eat at Castillo's without everyone talking? I cannot believe this town."

"Please. You were born and raised here. You know how it goes. Gossip spreads like a prairie fire."

"I should take out a billboard on Central Avenue. Two sentences. *I am not getting back together with Hayes Parker. We are just friends.* And then slap my signature on it."

Ice cubes rattled as Marisa sipped her tea. "That would definitely cause a stir. And then everyone could argue about whether or not it's the truth, and if it is, how long you two will *stay* just friends."

"It's ridiculous," Chrissy muttered under her breath.

Marisa spoke more gently, "It's reality is what it is."

"I promise you, I'm just staying at the ranch temporarily while my condo is being repaired. And I am sleeping *alone* in Rylee's old bedroom. I mean, how many times do I need to remind people of that?"

"Oh, let me think… Hundreds? Thousands? And they still won't believe you."

"You are not reassuring me."

Marisa set down her fork. "Are you really upset?" When Chrissy let out a pitiful whine, suddenly Marisa was the one pushing back her chair. She stepped around the small table. "Come here. Come on." Chrissy got up. Again, they hugged it out.

"Thanks," said Chrissy softly when they were both sitting down again. "I needed that."

"Whatever happens, I'm guessing you two have made peace about the past?"

Chrissy nibbled a bite of bread and suddenly felt a little bit better about everything. "You're right. We have."

"And that's a good thing."

"Yeah," Chrissy agreed. "It's a good thing. It really is." And a change of subject was in order. "What's the latest on Winona? Tell me she's back."

Ninety-seven-year-old Winona Cobbs, who now lived in Bronco, but who was famous all over Montana for her psychic abilities and her talent at matchmaking any number of happy couples, had vanished from Bronco a couple of weeks ago, right before her wedding to Stanley Sanchez. Stanley was eighty-seven and madly in love with his bride-to-be. Everyone said he was devastated to have lost her.

Marisa shook her head. "Nobody knows why or where she went. She's still gone. It's scary."

"Oh, no. I really thought she would have reappeared by now." Chrissy forced a smile. "But she will. I mean, we have to stay positive, right?"

"That's right," Marisa agreed.

"Promise you'll call me right away if you hear anything."

"You know I will."

"Thanks. And you're the first one I'll call if I have news about her." Chrissy offered more tea.

Marisa accepted a refill. They chatted about happier subjects after that.

When her friend left, Chrissy cleared off the table and tried not to worry about the famous missing psychic—or to let her mind wander to thoughts of Hayes Parker.

That night, Hayes sat across the kitchen table from Chrissy and wished he knew how to make things better between them. He couldn't figure out what to do to breach the wall of silence that separated them since the other night. Because he really did want to be her friend.

But friendship with her was no easy thing. As soon as they got closer, he just wanted to be closer still.

And the whole point, as they'd agreed Saturday night, was to keep their distance. Not getting too cozy was the main job—and that job didn't lend itself to a lot of casual, friendly interaction.

Apparently, she felt the same—that it wasn't safe to try being good buddies.

Or maybe she was just fed up with him and had zero desire to speak to him at all.

Whatever was going through her mind, she was extra quiet about it. So both of them ate dinner without saying much.

At least Arlen kept the conversation going. He praised the meal and discussed the new roof they would put on the barn as soon as all the materials he'd ordered arrived. Arlen had worked several years for a roofing contractor, so he knew his way around the job.

Every day now, Hayes thanked his lucky stars for Arlen. The man could work circles around most ranch hands, and he seemed to have a handle on just about every task Hayes threw at him. And if Arlen didn't know how to do something, he could usually figure it out.

No, Arlen wouldn't stay forever. He wanted his own land, and he was saving up, same as Hayes had, to make that happen. But until he decided it was time to move on, Hayes would be grateful for his skills, his willingness to work a long, hard day and his good humor that rarely flagged.

After dinner, Arlen suggested, "How 'bout a beer?"

"I'm in. Thanks."

They went out to the trailer, where they sat under the stars, sipping cans of Bud with Rayna at their feet.

"Want to talk about whatever's going on between you and that pretty woman back in the kitchen?" Arlen asked.

"No, I do not."

"Well, all right then. Just thought I'd make the offer."

"Thanks. No."

"So then, how's your dad doing?"

Not a question he was dying to tackle, either. But he did it anyway. "He's getting better very slowly. Which reminds me, I need to get over to Bronco for a visit."

"You really think he's doing okay?"

"I do. But I should check for myself. My mom says not to worry, that his recovery is just taking longer than usual, but he is getting better. Knowing my dad, it's probably his attitude. He wants out of there and he's stewing about it, lying awake nights worrying over all the things he can't do anything about instead of getting some rest."

"Go tomorrow."

Hayes hesitated. "I hate to leave you here to manage everything on your own."

"How long will you be gone?"

"Half a day."

"It's not a problem. You know damn well there's nothing around here I can't handle."

Hayes grinned. "Now that you mention it, I've noticed that."

"So go. I'll hold down the fort here. If I run into a problem I can't solve, I'll give you a call."

"Well, look who's here," said Lionel the next morning when Hayes entered his hospital room. The old man actually smiled. And he looked better, too, Hayes thought— thinner, both in the face and around the middle. His color had also improved.

The room had two hospital beds, one of which was empty. There was a curtain to pull for privacy when the other bed was occupied. Hayes noted the neatly made folding cot on his dad's side of the room. That must be where his mom slept. He asked, "Did Mom go home?"

Lionel nodded. "She left a half hour ago. You probably passed her on the highway. I think she and that ex-girlfriend of yours are in some kind of cooking competition."

That made Hayes smile. "Yep. Chrissy wants to do all the cooking to pay for her room at the house. Mom thinks the cooking is *her* job. I'll tell you this much, the deep freeze is filling up fast."

His dad actually laughed. "Sounds like a win-win to me."

Hayes put up both hands. "Hey, I try to stay out of it."

"Humph. Wise course of action." Lionel dipped his chin at the empty chair by the bed. "Sit down. Take a load off."

Hayes dropped into the chair. "So, Dad, how are you feeling?"

His dad heaved a long, weary sigh. "I keep telling the doctors to let me out of here. But they're still not ready to do what I say. I've got high levels of this and low levels of that. Who understands all the medical talk? Not me. I've lived my whole life taking care of business and suddenly a bunch of guys in white coats think it's their place to tell me what to do and how to do it. I should be up and seeing after things at home."

Hayes disagreed, but he didn't say so. So far, this conversation was going surprisingly well. He didn't want to set his dad off, so he kept his mouth shut.

Lionel wasn't fooled. The old man grunted. "Go ahead. Whatever you're thinking, spit it out."

Fair enough, then. "Look, Dad. You've come this far.

Just stay here until the doctors release you. Get well. The ranch will still be there when you get back."

The old man drew a slow, measured breath. "You sure about that?"

"Yeah, Dad. I am."

Lionel got that stubborn look, teeth gritted, eyes narrowed. But he didn't say anything. Hayes tried to think of a suitably bland topic that would not in any way get his father stirred up.

As the seconds ticked by, he heard a sound at the small, narrow window. A blue jay sat on a leafy branch just beyond the glass. The bird gave the window a peck and then tipped his crested head from side to side, as though completely bumfuzzled at the invisible barrier between outside and in.

"That damn bird shows up at least once a day," grumbled Lionel. "Pecks the window every time, too. Like it's new to him all over again that he can't just come through to the other side."

Hayes tried not to stare outright at his dad. He wasn't sure exactly what was going on here. Had his father actually changed? Because overall, they were having a civil conversation. They hadn't had one of those since Hayes was thirteen years old.

"Tell me the truth," his father said.

"About what?"

"A few years back, Braden told me you went to college."

"I got a two-year online degree in ranch management from Casper College in Wyoming."

"You went to college on the internet?"

"Yeah, Dad. I did."

"Well. Ain't that a kick in the head." Lionel seemed impressed. And then he said so. "Good for you, son."

"Thanks, Dad."

"Your mother says your school friends from town came to work the place with you three or four days running, that they pulled things together."

"They did. I'm grateful."

"She says now you've hired a hand. A damn good one, too."

"Yeah. Arlen's the best there is."

"Your mother tells me you really do have everything under control."

"I don't know that I'd go that far. But I think we're keeping on top of it, overall."

Lionel nodded. And then he scowled. "Norma has also informed me that she's paying the bills with her freedom money and there's not a damn thing I can do to stop her."

"She does seem pretty determined about that." Hayes made his voice carefully neutral. He watched the warring emotions battle it out on his father's road map of a face— love and pride, frustration and shame that his wife would be using her mother's dying gift to keep the ranch afloat.

"Well," said Lionel, "I'm just going to say this…"

Dread crept up Hayes's spine. Was this where the criticisms and demands started in?

"Son." His father's voice was thick and low. "I want you to know that I'm grateful." Was that the sheen of tears in the old man's eyes? "So damn grateful for all you're doing right now. I've spent years thinking I would never see your face again. And yet here you are, riding in just when things have gone from bad to worse to damn near impossible. I thank you for that. I truly do."

Hayes realized his mouth was hanging open. He shut it and swallowed. Hard. Was there hope for him and his father, after all? "Dad, I…"

Lionel stopped him by raising his hand, palm out. "Let me say my piece here?"

"Uh. Yeah, sure. Go ahead."

"It has occurred to me that I might have been too hard on you, and on your brothers, too—and you know what? Forget about might-have-been. I probably *was* too tough on you three. I mean, look at you. Gone at eighteen and staying gone for way too long. Now Braden's taken off, too, and I know I'm the main reason. As for Miles, he answered the call of duty, yeah. But he's still gone now, isn't he? Lying here in this bed, I've got all the time in the world to think about how I raised you boys and if I was in the wrong."

Hayes was starting to feel a bit misty-eyed. "Dad, I—"

That hand went up again. "Still not finished."

"Okay, Dad."

"Was I in the wrong? That's the question." Lionel paused and then announced, "The answer is no."

Hayes blinked. "No?"

"No." Lionel's lips twisted in a self-righteous sneer. "I was *not* too hard on you. Because life is tough, and a man needs to be tougher—and that's why I did what I had to do to make you boys ready to face all the crap this world is bound to throw at you. Because there is no free lunch, no big, fancy picnic and you boys needed to know that. You needed to understand that, to believe it way deep down in your bones and—"

"Dad, listen…"

Lionel leveled a furious glare on him. "Did I say I was finished? Because I'm not. I'm right about this and you need to realize how right I am. So as far as regrets go? Screw 'em. I raised you boys right, and I am not sorry about that. Not one bit, no, siree."

Disappointment. Hayes felt it like a hundred pounds of

concrete pressing down on his shoulders. *Here we go again*, he thought. Just like old times, with Lionel ranting on, endlessly repeating his self-righteous reasons for being a jerk.

Hayes should probably leave it alone, let the old man rant. But by then he was just fed up enough to fight back. "Come on, Dad. A kid needs more than mean words and ultimatums, more than warnings and constant reminders of how he's doing everything wrong. A kid needs love and respect. Everybody does. You seemed to understand that with Rylee—or at least, you didn't ride her constantly about every little thing."

"It's different with girls."

"How?"

"If you don't know, I'm certainly not going to tell you."

"You're dodging the question."

"The point is, I did respect you, damn it. I respected you enough to teach you how to be strong. I taught you to keep going no matter what, to do it right and if you do get it wrong, to keep trying, to find a way to obliterate every obstacle in your path. I taught you never to give up! And, son, look at you now. Right here in front of me today when fifteen years ago you swore I would never see your face again.

"You showed up when it mattered. You've got the grit to do what needs doing to save the ranch. And I am proud to say that you've got what it takes because I raised you right. I made it my mission never to let you get away with one damn thing and that made you strong!"

"You're shouting, Dad."

"Damn right I am! I have plenty to say, and I mean to say it!"

The door swung open. A nurse bustled in. "What is going on in here?" She turned to Hayes. "Step aside, please." Hayes moved away from the bed as the nurse marched straight for it, her eyes on Lionel now. "Mr. Parker, you need to keep it down. This is a hospital, and many of our patients are trying to rest. I can hear you all the way to the nurses' station."

"Humph," Lionel replied.

"Beyond the disturbance you're creating," the nurse said more gently, "it's just not good for you to get all worked up like this. Your blood pressure is spiking. You need to calm down."

There was a stare-down. Lionel glared at the petite gray-haired nurse and she glared right back at him.

Hayes's dad was the one who broke. "Sorry," he muttered. Suddenly, he looked bone tired, the shadows under his eyes darker than before. "Fine. I'll keep it down."

"Thank you." The nurse smiled sweetly, patted him on the shoulder, and left.

As the door swung shut behind her, Lionel turned his glare on Hayes. "Well." He spoke quietly, but with an underpinning of steel despite the exhaustion on his haggard face. "I had something to say, and I said it." He folded his arms across his barrel chest.

Hayes managed to shut his mouth before a bitter response escaped. There was no win in starting the argument all over again.

His dad taunted. "You think you got something to say back to me, go for it."

"There's no point."

"Because you've got nothing. You know I'm right."

"That's not true. I just don't think you're listening, Dad."

"Say it."

Hayes drew his shoulders back. "All right. It's just that I do believe it's possible to teach a kid how to survive without constantly yelling at him, pointing out every error he makes and reminding him over and over again of all the ways he's messed up."

"You're wrong. Just wait. You'll understand when you have sons of your own."

"You drove me away, Dad. And Braden, too. Probably Miles. Is that really what you wanted?"

His dad only shook his head, sank back against the pillow and closed his eyes.

Chapter Seven

That evening, it was just Chrissy and Hayes at the kitchen table for dinner. Arlen had gone into town to eat and most likely to visit the Grizzly.

Chrissy thought Hayes seemed thoughtful, and not really in a good way. Like he was stewing over something, trying to figure it out—and not getting anywhere. He'd mentioned at breakfast that he was driving over to Bronco to see his dad.

Had the visit gone wrong somehow? Probably. She wanted to ask Hayes about it. But the faraway look in his eyes discouraged conversation.

After the meal, he started to help her clean up. She shooed him away. "I've got this," she said, and took his dirty plate from him.

He gave her a half-hearted smile. "Have it your way." With Rayna close at his heels, he went out to take care of evening chores.

She cleaned up the kitchen, dusted the great room and then went upstairs to tweak a couple of menus for events in the coming weeks. It was almost dark when she finished but still too early to go to bed. Plus, she felt kind of edgy, like there was something she ought to be dealing with. She just didn't know what.

So she wandered back downstairs where all the rooms were empty. When she peeked through the window that looked out on the front porch, she saw Hayes sitting on the steps and Rayna in her usual spot, sprawled out behind him. His back was to her. She couldn't see his face.

But there was something in the set of his shoulders that spoke of discouragement. He was definitely feeling down.

She wanted to comfort him, though offering comfort didn't exactly go hand-in-hand with keeping her distance. After Saturday night, she did need to watch her step or she could end up getting something started that would not end well.

It was only…

He just seemed so sad sitting there. She couldn't even see his face, but his body language spoke of burdens too heavy to bear. She couldn't stop thinking that he needed a friend, someone to talk to, someone to listen to whatever he had on his mind.

Before she could remind herself again of all the reasons to turn around and head back up the stairs, she was pulling the front door open.

Hayes glanced over his shoulder and saw her standing in the open doorway. "What's up?"

"Want some company?"

Time stretched out. They just looked at each other. Finally, he patted the empty space beside him.

Pulling the door shut behind her, she dipped to give Rayna a pat on the head, then stepped over the dog to join him. For several minutes, not a word was said. They stared up at the dark, starry sky.

"Nice night," she said.

"Yeah. Warm. Not too windy."

She tried again. "I noticed all that stuff for the barn roof arrived today."

He nodded. "Arlen says that the two of us together can get that job done in two days."

"That's great."

"Yeah. Eventually, I might even look into hiring professionals to paint the barn and the house. Maybe next month. Depending on the cost. If it's too much, at some point I'll just buy the paint and do it myself."

"Ah," she replied. "New paint would really spruce up the place."

"Yeah," he said glumly.

"Hayes..."

"Huh?"

She looked into his clear green eyes and asked, "You okay?"

He made a low, thoughtful sound. "I've been better."

She waited. After all these years, she could still read him. Right now, she knew he needed a moment to decide how much he wanted to say to her. Behind them, Rayna shifted, her tags rattling.

Finally he spoke again. "It's my dad."

"Yeah. I kind of figured."

"Today, I thought for half a minute or so that maybe we were getting somewhere, taking the first steps toward making peace with each other. But then it was just the same old crap from him all over again. How he was tough on me and my brothers because we needed him to be a mean SOB so we could learn how to survive in the world."

"You're right," she said with a sigh. "That's nothing new."

"Exactly."

"But tell me about that half a minute when you thought you were getting somewhere."

He looked down at the porch step beneath his boots and then back up at her. "He thanked me—for coming back, and for taking care of the ranch while he's laid up."

"Well, that really is progress."

"Yeah. Maybe…" He stared out at the night, his lean jaw set.

She knew she should avoid touching him. But come on, they were friends now, and she wanted to comfort him. She clasped his arm. "I'm glad to hear that he praised you a little. He *should* praise you for the way you've taken things in hand here at the ranch. Especially given that he disinherited you when you dared to strike out on your own fifteen years ago."

He let out a short laugh. "Yeah, about that…"

"What about it?"

He met her eyes again. She was still holding on to his arm. She should let go. But she didn't. They shared a long look. A hot, prickly shiver ran up the backs of her knees. His gaze shifted a fraction. He was looking at her mouth—and now her lips were tingling.

He said, "Turns out, my dad never did change his will. My mom told me last week. She said it was all talk, that my dad never would do a thing like that."

"Oh, Hayes." Her throat felt tight. She gave a little cough to clear it. "I'm so glad to hear that."

He touched her cheek. His finger came away wet. "If you're glad, then why are you crying?"

She sniffed. "It's only a few tears. And they are tears of happiness. Your dad *is* a good man. He shouldn't have threatened you with losing your part of the ranch, but at least he didn't go through with it."

"Yeah. Still, I'm not really over how he let me *think* for all these years that he'd cut me out."

"I hear you. And I'm not saying that you *should* be over it."

"Thanks," he muttered, staring at the low shadowed humps of the gray hills way out there in the far distance.

"It's heartbreaking, the way your dad tries to be so tough and only ends up pushing people away."

"Heartbreaking? To you, maybe. As for me, well, his attitude just plain pisses me off."

She nudged him with her elbow. "You might be a little bit heartbroken about it, too."

He scoffed. "Fine. Maybe a little."

"And at least today he gave you credit for coming back, for taking things in hand here when there really was no one else to do it. It's a step in the right direction."

He gave a half shrug. "Yeah. I'll try to look at it that way."

She knew she shouldn't reach for his hand—but she did it anyway. When he didn't pull back, she laced her fingers with his. "You're a good guy," she reminded him. "And your dad knows it. I do believe that eventually he'll come around completely. The two of you will end up working together. Just wait and see."

He chuckled. "There you go, looking on the bright side."

"Yep." She gave his fingers a squeeze. "I am a cockeyed optimist and proud of it."

His gaze shifted from her eyes to her lips and back to her eyes again. Were her cheeks flushed? They did feel kind of warm... "You sound like *your* dad now," he said.

That made her smile. "You're right. It's one of his favorite expressions. Whenever Mom gives him a bad time for not facing reality as she sees it, he just grins and says he's a cockeyed optimist and she ought to be used to that by now."

"I used to wish that my dad could be like yours," he said, "always thoughtful and understanding. Plus, your dad has an actual sense of humor." Now his eyes were focused solely on her mouth.

She felt that focus in her belly, which was suddenly full of fluttery sensations. "Yeah," she said. "My dad's the best. Secretly, I think even my mom loves that he keeps things upbeat no matter what. She'd never admit it, though." Her voice sounded slightly breathless. Didn't it?

Because she certainly *felt* breathless. And those fluttery feelings in her belly? More so with every second that passed. He rubbed his rough thumb over the back of her hand. How could such a simple touch burn her all the way to the core?

Several seconds passed during which neither of them said a word.

By then, there was only his gaze holding hers, his thumb continuing its rough caress.

"Chrissy," he whispered, their faces so close now that their noses almost touched.

"Hmm?"

He moved then, leaning in that extra fraction of an inch, tipping his head just slightly so that their lips aligned.

"Hayes," she whispered as his mouth touched hers.

And then his strong arms were around her. She melted into him.

Now there was nothing but his mouth on hers, nothing but the taste of him, clean and sweet and so well remembered.

Her yearning had a pulse, and her heart was a wild thing, pounding away at the cage of her ribs.

When he pulled back, she almost slid her hands up over his chest, almost wrapped them around his neck, almost yanked him back down to her. Almost.

But not quite.

Instead, she drew a slow, careful breath and opened her eyes.

His were waiting. Slowly, as though afraid any sudden move might spook her, he touched her cheek. Catching a loose curl of her hair, he guided it back behind her ear. "There I go." His voice was deeper than ever right then, dark as the shadows in his eyes. "Stepping over the line again…"

She laughed low. "It's not like I resisted or asked you to stop."

"Chrissy, we had an agreement."

"Yes, Hayes. I am aware."

"And now I've broken it."

"Oh, yes, you did."

"And you know what?"

She shook her head slowly. "Tell me."

"Now I just want to break it all over again."

"Do you see me stopping you?" She was whispering now.

"So, then…?"

She knew it was her move. And she made it. Surging up, she pressed her parted lips to his.

He gathered her in with a groan.

That kiss went on forever. It was so good, so sweet and so tender. So wild. Just what she needed right now—to be wanted as only Hayes had ever wanted her. To be swept away to that place where all the everyday stuff just didn't matter at all.

When she got lost in his kiss, there was only right now.

Too bad they couldn't just sit here on the front step and keep kissing forever.

She opened her eyes to find him watching her. When she pulled back enough to give him a wobbly smile, he released her. She faced the front walk again, but then his arm came around her. She settled against his side, resting her head on his shoulder.

His lips brushed her hair. She felt the warmth of his breath as he whispered, "So much for the friendship plan."

"Hey." She lifted a hand and patted his chest. "We're still friends. I promise."

"I'm glad." He sounded sincere. "Too bad I have so much trouble keeping my hands off of you."

"Same." She tipped her head up to him. His eyes were jewel-green now. She asked, "What are we going to do about this problem of ours?" When he frowned but failed to answer, she made herself offer, "If you want me to move out, just say so."

His arm tightened around her. "I don't. Uh-uh. Please don't move out, Chrissy."

"You're serious?"

"Oh, yeah. No way am I kicking you out. You carry your weight. And you're right there to listen to me gripe on endlessly about my dad. Having you here just makes everything better. You cheer me up, you really do."

Warmth spread through her at his praise. "Thank you."

"So then, stick with the plan. Stay until your condo's ready for you."

She drew a slow breath as she gathered her courage. "Hayes. We have to get real here. Promising to keep our distance isn't working."

"I know."

She made herself put it right out there. "I just have to say, if this goes where it feels like it's going and we end up in bed together, you should know it can only be for now. Because my life? It's kind of a mess. I'm not at a place where I can take on a relationship."

"I get it. I do. And as for your life being a mess, you're not the only one."

"Hayes, we can be friends. We can…consider adding

benefits. But I'm not ready in any way for more than that. I'll say it again to drive the point home. It can only be for now."

He held her closer. "I can't believe you just said it out loud."

"That it's only for now?"

"No. The part about adding benefits."

She ordered the butterflies in her belly to settle down and answered him honestly. "Well, we can't just pretend that it's all buddy-buddy between us—and keep letting ourselves share the kind of kisses that could burn this house down."

"I hear you. And you don't have to worry. If it gets out of hand, we're agreed on where we stand about the future."

"Yeah." She swallowed hard. "There is no future for you and me."

He nodded. "You're not ready for more and I never will be."

She pulled away from the shelter of his arm, just enough to look him in the eye. "Never? Are you serious?"

"Yeah," he said in a gruff voice. "Losing you almost broke me. And then when Anna died… Well, it was bad. Really bad. We had so many plans, me and Anna. And all of them were wiped out by a patch of black ice on a cold December night. I can't do it again, Chrissy. I'm through with falling in love. I just don't have another damn heartbreak in me."

She wanted to argue—that he shouldn't completely give up on love. That someday he *would* be ready again. That love didn't always end in heartbreak.

But for him—and for her, too—it had. And she knew him well enough to know that he meant what he said. Plus, she was staring right into his eyes. She saw nothing but brutal honesty there. Steering clear of love was his choice and she needed to respect that.

"You have that look," he said with a crooked smile. "The one that says it's time to call it a night."

Her throat had clutched up again. "I just don't have the words, that's all. I haven't had much luck with love, either. But still, for me, the way love has ended has always been a matter of choices—between you and me. And then between me and Sam. In both of those relationships, it ended with both of us still standing. It ended because it had become impossible to stay together.

"But you and Anna, you didn't get a choice and you didn't get all that long together, either. That just feels so completely wrong. I can understand why you don't want to go there ever again. I don't like it. And I'm sad for you. But I get it. I do." She stood.

He lifted his head to meet her eyes. "You're going in?"

"Yeah." She stepped over Rayna and went to the door. "Night, Chrissy."

"Night." She turned and left him there.

Hayes watched the door close behind her and had to actively resist the need to jump up and follow her, to catch hold of her hand, pull her close again, wrap his arms around her good and tight.

They really weren't going anywhere together. They'd been done for a long, long time.

He wanted her, yeah. He wanted her a lot. He wanted her for as long as it lasted. And he knew that couldn't be for very long.

But he didn't want to hurt her the way he'd hurt her in the past. They were on good terms now. Bringing sex into it could blow everything to hell all over again.

So he waited out there in the dark for another hour, long enough to be certain that when he went inside, she would be upstairs in her bedroom with the door firmly shut.

"Good morning!" Chrissy announced way too brightly when Hayes and Arlen came in from the barn at seven a.m. the next day. "Ready for breakfast?" she chirped.

"I sure am!" Hayes ladled on the enthusiasm. To Chrissy, it sounded phony as hell. And that was just fine. The phonier the better. They would stomp out any promise of intimacy by faking friendliness for all they were worth.

They ate. Hayes told her that her biscuits and gravy rivaled his mom's.

She blasted him her brightest smile. "High praise! I'll take it!"

At dinner, he said her pork chops couldn't be beat. When he asked her about work, she beamed and announced it was, "Fine. Just fine!"

They spent a full five minutes on the weather—hot, with no chance of rain, just like every day in Tenacity, Montana, during the month of August. Then Hayes bragged about the progress he and Arlen had made toward getting the new roof on the barn. "Looks like we really will finish tomorrow."

"That's terrific!" she exclaimed.

Arlen hardly said a word through the meal. He watched Hayes and Chrissy as they alternately ate in painful silence and lobbed meaningless phrases at each other in ridiculously cheerful voices.

"Beer?" Arlen asked Hayes cautiously when dinner was finished.

"You're on," Hayes replied, grateful for a reason to get out of that kitchen and away from the woman he needed *not* to get close to.

They were sitting out under the sky by the trailer, Buds in hand, Rayna snoozing on the grass between them when Arlen said, "What the hell's going now between you and Chrissy?"

Had Hayes known that was coming? Pretty much. "Nothing," he lied through his teeth.

Arlen wasn't buying. "You guys were getting close—and suddenly, you're making fake noises and wearing phony smiles."

"Who said we were getting close?"

Arlen enjoyed a long sip of beer. "If you're not going to answer my question, just say so."

Hayes said nothing for several long seconds. Arlen waited him out. Finally, Hayes explained, "Yeah. Me and Chrissy had a talk last night. Neither of us wants to get involved right now. So we're trying to keep things casual and no more than friendly, you know?"

"And you don't want to get involved, why?"

Hayes crushed his empty can and dug in the cooler for another. "She's not ready for anything serious and I'm never getting serious again. So it's better if we keep our distance."

Arlen frowned. "I don't get it. But hey. If you say so…"

"What's not to get? We're both just being careful not to start something we can't finish."

"So then, you got something sweet between you, but your plan is to pretend you don't."

"We're friends, okay? And we want to keep it that way."

Arlen put up a hand. "Enough. Do it like you need to do it."

"What does that mean?"

"It means that you want her, and she wants you and you're not hiding how you feel about each other with all those fake smiles you two keep dishing out."

Hayes said nothing for a long count of ten. Finally, he stretched his legs out in front of him and leaned back to stare up at the stars that were getting brighter as the night came on. "We're both just doing the best we can."

"I get that. On the other hand, why not just go with it, see how it shakes out?"

"Because the result could be a whole lot of heartbreak. I've had plenty of that—more than my share."

"You can't win the lottery if you never buy a ticket."

"Arlen."

"Yeah?"

"Just drink your beer."

His friend shook his head, but he did let it go.

The next morning as he helped Chrissy clear off the breakfast dishes, she said she would be having dinner at her parents' house. She went on, "But thanks to your mom, there's enough to feed an army in the freezer. Most of it's already packaged in serving-size portions. Pick out what you're in the mood for and stick it in the microwave."

Hayes watched her lips move as she talked and tried not to picture himself just grabbing her and slamming his mouth down on hers. "I think we can handle it."

"Great," she said glumly.

He knew that expression. "Your mom giving you grief again?"

"Not right this minute, no." She tipped her head down.

He resisted the need to put a finger under her chin and guide her head up so she would look at him some more. "But you have a feeling she will be when you see her tonight?"

Her answer was a tiny shrug.

He said, "She loves you and she means well."

She lifted her head then. Their eyes met again. Bam! Like a punch to the gut. "Yep." She forced a bright grin.

It took every ounce of will he possessed not to pull her close and kiss her.

Denial and bright smiles just weren't working.

He didn't know how long he could continue to resist the need to grab her close and hold on tight. He didn't really even want to resist. He wanted to give in, just let it happen and hope for the best when the end came.

That day, Hayes and Arlen hit their goal. By the time they finished work that evening, the barn was looking a whole lot better due to the new roof.

Back at the house, Hayes didn't even bother to check the deep freeze. He decided to get out and go somewhere noisy where there was beer. Arlen said he was up for that, too. Hayes called his buddies. Austin was out of town, but Jake and Beck agreed to meet them at the Grizzly.

The bar was doing a brisk business for a Thursday night in their small, dusty town. They ordered some pitchers, played eight-ball and listened to ancient country on the equally antique jukebox.

A couple of women Hayes vaguely remembered from high school came in about eight. Jake must have seen the frown on his face as he tried to remember their names.

"Lana Colby and Kerry Fox," Jake said, leaning close to be heard over a Tammy Wynette song. "They were two years behind us at Tenacity High."

"Right. I remember now. They were best friends even back then, joined at the hip."

"Yep. Kerry's never tied the knot. But Lana got married right after high school. Her divorce was final last year, so she's a Colby again."

"Gotcha." It was more than Hayes really needed to know.

Lana and Kerry joined in taking their turns at eight-ball with the guys. Kerry was kind of shy. But Lana knew how to handle a pool cue. She was also a world-class flirt.

When Hayes squeaked out a win on her, she batted her eyelashes and grinned. "I think you owe me a beer, Hayes Parker."

Hayes frowned. "Wait a minute. Didn't I just win?"

"And so you buy me a beer. That's how it works." She sidled in close and nudged him with her elbow as she dished out a teasing smile.

He bought her a beer. She thanked him with way more enthusiasm than the gesture required. And after that, every time he looked up from the pool table, she was giving him the come-and-get-it eyes.

At one point, Arlen muttered out of the side of his mouth, "That girl has a goal and I do believe that you are it."

"Well, that's not going to happen."

Arlen clapped him on the shoulder and then bent to make a shot.

Hayes spent the rest of the evening avoiding eye contact with Lana Colby and trying really hard not to wonder how Chrissy was holding up at her mother's house.

"I haven't heard from Sam." Chrissy's mom cut a bite of herb-crusted lamb chop and then added glumly, "I suppose I didn't really expect to."

Chrissy nibbled at an asparagus spear. It hadn't surprised her in the least that Sam had sent her mom a chain of postcards. He'd always liked her mom. Patrice was very much like Sam's mother, a pretty woman who stayed home and took care of her family and had no desire to get out and mix it up in the workaday world. "Looks like Sam is moving on, Mom."

"Yes." Patrice sighed. "I suppose it's for the best."

"Probably."

"Do you miss him at all?"

Chrissy set down her fork and sipped her ice water. The person she missed was Hayes. They'd spent the past two days speaking to each other in short sentences, trying to be cheerful and ending up just being weird.

It wasn't going well. Not for her, anyway. If he avoided her, she felt bereft. And when he was sweet and understanding—like this morning when he asked her if everything was okay with her mom and then listened to her answer with understanding in his eyes—it took monumental effort not to fling herself into his arms.

Maybe she really should move out now.

Too bad she couldn't bear the thought of that, though she knew very well that it was going to happen soon enough anyway.

No doubt about it. She was living in a fool's dream.

"Chrissy? I asked you a question."

"Hmm?"

"Honestly." Her mother pursed her lips in disapproval. "I'll ask again. Don't you miss Sam at all?"

"Miss him?"

"Well? Do you?"

Chrissy tried to answer honestly. "Mom, I loved Sam. It didn't work out. We got divorced. Yes, for a while I was sad, and I really did miss him then. But that feeling has faded. Now I only wish him well."

Her mom just looked at her, like she couldn't figure out what in the world to say to that.

Chrissy's dad came to the rescue. "I stopped in at your place today. They're making good progress on the repairs."

"Yes." Chrissy beamed him a grateful smile. "It's going

well. I should be able to move back in sometime in the next month or so."

Her mom smiled then. "Your father says insurance is going to cover everything."

She nodded. "Yeah. It looks like it. And I'm so grateful for that." Which had her wondering, if she did decide she really needed to put some distance between her and Hayes, how much of a housing reimbursement would she get? She should check into that.

"I'm just going to say it one more time." Her mom glanced down as she smoothed the napkin on her lap. "We would love to have you come stay with us until your place is ready."

"Thanks, Mom," she answered automatically. "I appreciate that."

"So then you'll think about it?"

She would definitely be checking into what her insurance would cover first. As for her mom's question, agreeing to *think about* staying here for a month would only have Patrice redoubling her efforts to get Chrissy to follow through. She just didn't want to do that if she could possibly avoid it.

"It's working out beautifully at the Parker ranch," she shamelessly lied. "So for now, I'm staying put."

"But you *will* think about it." Her mom wore her sweetest smile.

And Chrissy gave in enough to agree, "Of course."

When she got back to the ranch that night, Hayes's pickup was nowhere in sight and Rayna was waiting at the gate inside the fence that surrounded the yard.

"Hey, girl." She crouched to greet the big dog. "How's it going?"

Rayna panted with happiness as Chrissy gave her a good scratch along her back to her furry tail and also behind the ears. The dog followed her up to the porch. It was a warm, windless night, so Chrissy sat on the step the way she had with Hayes two nights before. With a big yawn, Rayna plopped down behind her.

Ten minutes later, Chrissy was still sitting there thinking that she would get up and go inside any minute now. But she didn't. She stared out at the night for another half hour and tried not to wonder where Hayes had gone off to.

Tenacity was a very small town and there weren't that many options for nighttime entertainment. So yeah, probably the Grizzly. She propped her elbows on her knees and her chin on the heel of her hand and hated herself for picturing him picking up some pretty woman and letting her take him home.

"It would be better if he just went ahead and did that." She hadn't realized she'd said it out loud until Rayna gave a little whine.

"Sorry, girl." She reached back and stroked Rayna's head to reassure her that all was well with the world.

Even if it wasn't. Even if Chrissy felt like a hopeless fool.

After twenty more minutes had staggered by, she got up to go in. She would have taken Rayna with her, but the dog wouldn't cross the threshold.

"Okay, girl." Chrissy bent to give her a quick hug. "You go ahead and wait for him."

Inside, she went straight up the stairs to her room, changed into a big, soft sleep shirt and padded down the hall to brush her teeth. She'd just climbed into bed and turned off the lamp when she heard faint sounds outside.

And she knew.

He was home.

Downstairs, the front door opened and closed.

Not that she cared. She didn't. Not one bit.

With a huff of annoyance, she pulled the blankets up over her head like some scared little girl hiding from a bad dream in the middle of the night. She shut her eyes and breathed slow and deep and told herself she didn't care if he'd gone and brought some other woman home with him.

Hayes could do what he wanted to do.

They were not getting anything started between them, and if she ended up feeding breakfast to some buckle bunny tomorrow morning, well, wouldn't that just be for the best?

At least it would serve as a reminder that getting involved with Hayes Parker all over again would be the ultimate in unacceptable choices. And it might even give her the nudge she needed to talk to her insurance agent about her relocation allotment.

There were boots on the stairs, but she didn't hear voices.

So what? Voices or not, it didn't matter. She was never going to go there. Uh-uh. Hayes Parker was off-limits. The two of them were never, ever, ever going to happen again.

Chapter Eight

In the morning, it was just Hayes, Arlen and Chrissy at the breakfast table. If Hayes had brought home a woman, she'd left well before dawn.

Hayes kept looking at her funny. She mostly tried *not* to look at him. Once or twice, Arlen made the effort to start an actual conversation. Neither Chrissy nor Hayes responded.

She had no interest in chitchat right now. She wanted Hayes but she wasn't going to have him, so the best thing for her in this moment was to eat her food, clean up after the meal and get ready for work. No cheerful breakfast chatter. It would only have her letting down her guard, opening herself up to the temptation to put a move on the man sitting to her right at the table.

Hayes was equally silent that morning. He ate his biscuits and gravy and gave Arlen one-word replies whenever the other man asked him a direct question. It shouldn't have been that hard for Chrissy to completely ignore him.

Oh, but it was hard. Her gaze kept trying to stray his way.

When the two men finally went back out to work, she didn't know whether she felt relieved or deeply depressed.

At the inn, things went pretty well. She had two back-to-back luncheons to deal with but nothing any later in the day. She checked out at a little after four. There were no events scheduled for Saturday or Sunday. The weekend stretched out ahead of her, feeling empty. Endless.

Hanging around at the ranch trying to avoid Hayes didn't sound like a whole lot of fun. Maybe she'd drive over to Bronco, do a little shopping, treat herself to an overnight stay at a nice hotel. That could be fun. Maybe.

At least in Bronco, she wouldn't have to lie in bed trying not to listen for the sounds of Hayes's pickup pulling in out front.

On the way home, she went to Tenacity Grocery and picked up a few things. From there, she drove to her condo, which still looked a million years from completion. But progress was being made. Eventually, she would have her home back.

By then it was a little after five. She decided to stop in and check with her insurance agent. Yes, he said, she could claim reimbursement for lodging until her condo was move-in ready. He gave her paperwork to submit when she found a place.

By the time she got back into her Blazer again, it was after six. Reluctantly, she returned to the ranch.

Hayes had left her a note on the kitchen table. Arlen was having dinner in town and Hayes had driven over to Bronco to visit his dad. Apparently, he'd taken Rayna with him. The dog was nowhere to be seen.

Chrissy heated up some leftovers and ate them standing at the sink, staring out the window toward the barn, feeling uncomfortable inside her own skin.

She needed to get out, move around. Upstairs, she changed into jeans, a T-shirt and sturdy boots and went for a walk on one of the dirt roads that crisscrossed the End of the Road Ranch.

She kept going until she came to a lone hackberry tree.

Ducking in under the branches, she sat down with her back against the trunk. A few yards away, beyond a barbwire fence, cattle grazed peacefully.

It did kind of clear her head a bit, just to sit here, alone in the shade of a tree, staring off past the grazing cattle toward the wide-open prairie rolling forever toward the distant hills. The feeling that she might just burst right out of her skin faded a bit. And her unreasonable anger with Hayes faded to a low hum beneath her breastbone. Really, she had no reason to be angry with him.

He didn't want to get anything started when he knew it would go nowhere. She could respect that. She *did* respect that. And from now on, whenever she had to deal with him, she would be civil and casually friendly.

It would all work out. And if it didn't, she would find herself another place to stay. There was no big emergency. She just needed to take things day-to-day.

The light was fading fast, the air cooling off as she rose and started toward the house. It was a long walk back, and by the time she let herself in the front gate, the sky was a star-thick indigo bowl overhead—and Hayes sat on the step as he had two nights before, with Rayna snoozing behind him.

She went in the gate, and he rose, six-foot-two of lean, hard cowboy, in faded jeans, his usual worn boots and T-shirt. He had on a black leather jacket, too. It looked vintage, like something a brooding fifties movie star might wear.

At the foot of the steps, she paused, feeling awkward and out of place, not knowing what to say, but not willing to be outright rude and simply dodge around him.

Forking his fingers through his unruly hair, he smiled down at her. "Hey."

She felt her own mouth tipping up in answer. "Hey."

"I got a little worried about you. Your Blazer was here and you weren't."

"I'm good. Just went for a walk."

"Ah."

"Yeah. I found a tree to sit under. I watched the cattle graze and stared at the mountains off in the distance. It was nice. Kind of soothing after a long day at the inn."

Okay, it was a lie. Her workday had been uneventful. She'd gone for a walk to try to clear her mind—of him. And why did he just stand there above her, looking down at her as though he was waiting for her to make some kind of move?

When she couldn't stand the silence for one more second, she said the first thing that popped into her mind. "Nice jacket."

"You like it?"

"I do. You've got kind of a James Dean thing going on wearing that."

He smirked. "Found it at a flea market in Boise ten or twelve years ago."

"Ah." And so much for the history of his flea-market jacket. She stuck her hands in her pockets. "Well, I guess I'll just go on in then."

He tipped his head and gave her a long, steady look. "Sit with me." Her hopeless heart skipped a beat and then started racing. She mentally ordered it to slow the heck down as she opened her mouth to say she really needed to go in.

He must have guessed what she was about to say from the look on her face because he coaxed, "Just for a little while."

"Why not?" She stared into those jade eyes of his and heard herself echo, "Just for a little while."

He scooted to the side and she took the empty space next to him. "I have news," he said.

Rayna gave a little whine of hello. Chrissy turned to her and patted her head. "Hey, girl..."

"My dad's coming home tomorrow."

"Wow. That's great news."

"Yeah. His test results are better. He's lost a lot of weight and things are looking pretty good. Now, if the two of us can just keep from killing each other..."

"Don't even start in with that. You'll work it out."

"Yeah, probably with our fists."

That didn't sound good. She sat up straighter. "What do you mean? He never used to hit you. Where is this coming from?"

His strong shoulders slumped. "No, he never hit me."

"So you were just being a smart-ass, then?"

"He and I don't get along, Chrissy. It's a fact."

She put her hand on his knee and then almost jerked it back. But she wanted to reassure him. So she gave that hard knee a squeeze and bumped his arm gently with her shoulder—and then she let go. "I'm thinking we should plan a low-key celebration of his return. Maybe a welcome-home barbecue on Sunday. We can invite Beck, Jake and Austin in thanks for how they helped you out. And Arlen. Rylee and Shep, of course. Just a small get-together, not a big deal."

"I don't know if that's a good idea. He's been really sick. I mean, he *is* better, but I don't think he's ready to party."

"If he gets tired, he can go to bed. Everyone will understand. But I think it's nice to make a little fuss, to make it clear how glad we are that he's pulling through."

"Yeah, but what if he acts up?"

"We can take it. We'll just keep on smiling. Besides, it

will be worth putting up with a little attitude from him for the chance to show him that we're glad to have him home."

He looked at her for the longest time.

Finally, she had to ask, "What are you staring at?"

"You."

"Why?"

"You get ideas. And then you get all excited about them. Remember prom? You were on the planning committee. The theme was Starry Night. Twinkle lights everywhere and a giant moon suspended from the blue velvet ceiling."

"I was proud of how those decorations turned out."

"You were obsessed."

"Fine. I was obsessed. And the grange hall was the best it's ever looked. It was absolutely stunning, as you well know."

"You were the stunning one. In that blue satin dress."

Her cheeks felt too warm, and her heart had found a faster rhythm. She reminded herself that she was no longer some giddy high school girl, getting all excited because Hayes Parker called her stunning. "Thank you. And please don't try to change the subject. Just say yes to the barbecue. You'll have to handle the grill, but I'll take care of everything else."

He scoffed, but in a playful way. "Don't kid yourself. My mom will be here, remember? She will never allow you to do everything on your own. She will pitch in no matter how many times you tell her to stop."

"I love your mom. I also realize there is no way in heaven to keep Norma Parker from pitching in—and making all the major decisions. So no worries, I'm good with that."

"How about you? Anyone you want to invite?"

"Hmm. Maybe Marisa Sanchez—you remember her?"

"Yeah. Invite Marisa."

"And there's Ruby McKinley. She works the front desk at the inn. She and I are getting close, becoming friends. She's a single mom with a little girl."

"Ask her to come—and her little girl, too."

"All right. I will."

"You should invite your mom and dad, too."

She blinked at him. "You're joking."

"No, I'm serious. Invite them."

"That could be a recipe for disaster," she warned—and then marveled at her own sudden lightheartedness. Somehow, all of her hurt and anger at him for ghosting her the past two days had vanished like fog in the light of the sun. She really needed to watch herself with him. He ran hot and cold. He would end up hurting her if she didn't keep her wits about her.

But it was hard to be wary when he looked at her with admiration, when he teased her about the good times back when they were together.

Maybe all she needed to do when it came to Hayes was to lighten up a little, kind of take things as they came.

"Come on," he teased. "Make the deal."

"There's a deal?"

"That's right. I'm all in on the barbecue as long as you ask your folks to come."

"I still don't get it. Why, exactly, do you want them here?"

"Why not include them? That's all I'm saying."

She had no comeback for that. Because he had a point. Back in high school, her parents had warned her off Hayes at first because of his reputation as a troublemaker. But he'd set out to charm them and he'd succeeded. Also, her parents had always been friendly with Hayes's mom and dad. Really, inviting her folks to join the welcome-home celebration would be a nice gesture.

"Shake on it." Hayes stuck out his hand.

She took it, but cautiously. His warm fingers closed around hers and a shiver of something dangerous skated up her arm. "Hayes?"

He didn't let go. "I've been thinking of only two things since the other night."

"What two things?" It came out sounding as wary as she felt.

He leaned close and whispered in her ear, "That I want to. But we shouldn't. But I want to. But we can't…"

Her heart melted, which thoroughly annoyed her. She pulled her hand from his. "You've been cold to me." The accusation came out on a husk of breath.

"I was trying to stay away."

"Oh, no kidding." Her tone was all sarcasm.

"I thought it would be better to back off, put some distance between us. But I can see now I just came off like a jerk."

"You're right. You did."

"I'm sorry."

She still wasn't ready to let it go. "Did you have fun at the Grizzly last night?"

He looked right in her eyes. "I had a couple of beers, played some pool and came home. Alone."

She believed him. Maybe she shouldn't. But she did. He took her hand again. She let him. "So what now?"

"Well, that's up to you. What do you think?"

"I think that look in your eye ought to be illegal."

"Chrissy." He said it low, with heat and clear intention.

If she said yes, it would be with no hope of forever. And she'd always been a forever kind of girl.

But maybe it was time to try something different, to go just a little bit wild.

She asked, "Just for now? That *is* what we're talking about here?"

His nod was slow and serious. "Yeah. Can you work with that?"

She was going to get hurt. She knew it like she knew every street and narrow sidewalk of the small, dusty town she'd grown up in. She was going to get hurt and that wasn't going to stop her from having him again.

"Just for now," she said firmly. "Yes. I can deal with that."

Like a punch to the solar plexus, those words of hers hit him hard. *Yes. I can deal with that.*

He let go of her hand—but only to wrap his arm around her shoulders and pull her close against his body. "Chrissy..." Breathing in her scent, he nuzzled her hair. She smelled so good, dewy and sweet. She always had. Like a tropical flower magically blooming on dry, barren land.

He took her mouth. She sighed as she opened for him. He tasted her deeply, his mind full of tender memories.

Their first time, fumbling in his pickup under a tall cottonwood by the creek that meandered across a wide stretch of Parker land. The full moon shining down on them through the dust-covered windshield. Her eyes in the darkness of the cab, looking up at him with love and trust.

He'd broken that trust. And now he was setting them up to break it all over again.

But resisting his need for her? A man couldn't turn down clear, cool water in the desert. A thirst like his would not be denied.

She threaded her fingers into the hair at his nape, grabbing, pulling a little. He groaned.

And she giggled. He kissed that little laugh right off her lips, nudging her to open for him.

Kissing Chrissy.

Nothing like it ever in this big, hard world.

All the years apart and now here they were, hot and heavy as ever, holding on tight, letting the need between them have control.

"Upstairs," he said, catching her lower lip between his teeth, teasing it until she moaned.

"My room." She sighed. "It's got the bigger bed."

He saw no reason to argue. There were twin beds in the room where he slept. "Let's go." He got his legs under him and stood, pulling her right up with him.

Now they were on their feet but going nowhere. The moon, half full, hovered above them as he kissed her some more, long and deep and hungrily.

She pushed at his shoulders with another light, happy laugh. "Are we just going to stand here kissing all night?"

He caught her face between his hands. "The idea holds definite appeal."

She turned her head enough to press a soft kiss into the heart of his left hand. "A bed. Doesn't that sound wonderful?"

"Now that you mention it…" He scooped her up. She wrapped her arms around his neck as he cradled her against his chest. "Let's go."

He carried her to the door. She pushed it open. Rayna wiggled in ahead of them.

Inside, she shoved the door shut and engaged the lock. "Put me down. I can walk up the stairs."

"Uh-uh." He held her a little bit tighter. "I'm not letting go of you until I have you where I want you."

She touched his mouth. "You sound so determined."

"You have no idea." He started walking.

At the top of the stairs, he paused.

She laughed. "Out of breath?"

"No way. I'm tough."

"Right." Her dark eyes were softer now. "You are the toughest."

"But I need to make a little detour."

"To…?"

He was already moving again. "My room. For condoms." Yeah, she'd said that she and Sam couldn't have children. But the way he saw it, even if there was no chance of her getting pregnant tonight, they might as well just play it safe.

The door to his room was open. He set her down on the threshold. "Stay right there. Don't move."

"I wouldn't dare."

"Good." He got his duffel and took what he needed from an inside pocket. When he got back to the doorway, she was already turning to walk to her room at the end of the hall. "Oh, no, you don't." He picked her up.

She wrapped her arm around his neck again and whispered in his ear, "I wasn't trying to get away."

He turned his head and kissed her hard and quick. "Yeah, well, I'm taking no chances."

A minute later, he entered the bedroom at the end of the upstairs hall. By then, his heart was running riot inside his chest—and not because he'd just carried her up the stairs and down the hall.

It was Chrissy that had his heart going wild—having Chrissy in his arms again.

After all these years.

Carefully, he set her down on the rag rug by the double bed.

"Oh, Hayes…" She put her hands on his shoulders and then slid them around his neck. "Hayes…" Lifting up, she touched her mouth to his.

That was all it took. He urged her to open and when she did, he kissed her hard and deep, gathering her into him, falling into the kiss, thinking that this couldn't be happening.

Oh, but it was.

Her hands were all over him, shoving his jacket off his shoulders, getting hold of his T-shirt. Her fingers skimmed along his sides. "Arms up." She kissed the words onto his mouth.

He did as she instructed, and the shirt went sailing back over her shoulder. She got to work on his belt buckle.

About then, he realized that she was still wearing all her clothes. He got down to business, tugging her T-shirt over her head, reaching around behind her and unhooking her lacy pink bra. The clasp fell away. He slid his hands up over the cool, silky skin of her back to hook his fingers under her bra straps.

A second later, that bra went flying toward the corner chair. She laughed and he kissed her. She tasted so good. Like all the beautiful things a man could lose forever—and then, by some miracle, find again.

For now, anyway. For now, he could hold her, touch her, kiss her. She was right here in his arms, and she was even more beautiful than all those years ago.

He cradled her pale, round breasts in his hands. "So pretty..." And he flicked the dusky nipples, his mind thrown back to their second time. In the bed of that old pickup he used to drive then.

"Remember, that night in the bed of your rusty old pickup?" she asked, as though she'd read his mind. "It was August, same as now, and hot. We parked under that giant cottonwood tree again, just miles from nowhere..."

Lost in her big brown eyes, he guided a long swatch of

shining hair behind the shell of her ear. "I will never forget it."

"That was something, all those soft old quilts and comforters piled up in the pickup bed. We made love, and then we just hung out there, whispering together, staring up the moon through the leaves of that cottonwood."

"It was a good night."

"The *best* night." She laughed softly. "All that bedding, soft as a cloud. Heaven, that's what it was, just lying there together, you and me."

He smiled, remembering back to that summer so long ago. Recalling how, earlier that day, he'd waited until the house was empty. Then he'd run up to the attic. It had taken more than one frantic trip up and down the stairs to gather the old quilts and comforters his mom kept tucked in a couple of big trunks up there. He was so sure he'd be caught.

But he got lucky—twice. Because he also had to get all that bedding back where it came from before the next morning so no one would know what he and Chrissy had been up to out in the far pasture after dark.

Now he was smirking. Because the truth was, he'd gotten lucky more than twice if you counted him and Chrissy under the cottonwood that night.

"It was good—so good." She had his belt off and she was sliding his zipper down. Slipping her hand under the elastic of his briefs, she closed her fingers around him.

"It was perfect." He groaned against her parted lips as she stroked him. But then he caught her wrist. "Let's get everything off. Now."

She threw back her head, her dark waterfall of hair swaying as she laughed. "Good plan."

He took the condoms from his pocket and set them on the little table by the bed. Two minutes later their clothes littered the floor, and they stood in the middle of the rug, naked, grinning at each other like a couple of naughty children.

"Well," she said, sounding breathless, her soft cheeks flushed, so beautiful it hurt just to look at her. "Here we are again."

He wasn't grinning now. "I missed you," he said, though he knew he shouldn't. Because they had an agreement. This was just for right now. Dangerous words should be scrupulously avoided.

But now those words had somehow gotten out of his mouth, and she looked stricken. "Please don't, Hayes."

He reached for her, took her hand, pulled her close and wrapped his arms around her good and tight. "Sorry." And oh, did she feel good, all soft and sleek and curvy, pressed right up against him. She made him ache for her.

She always had.

And then she tipped her head back, offering that beautiful mouth again. "Just kiss me. It's all right. We both want this and it's all right."

He did kiss her, a deep kiss that went on forever as he pulled her backward at the same time. They fell across the bed. Rolling her beneath him, he caught her wrists in either hand, pushing them out to the sides until her arms were stretched wide.

When he lifted his mouth, she said, "You know I can hardly move like this."

He nodded. "And that is exactly my plan." He kissed her some more. She sighed against his mouth as she tugged on her captured wrists—but not too hard, just enough to make them both smile.

In time, he moved lower. He scattered kisses over her pretty chin and down the satin skin of her throat.

Her breasts tempted him, so he lingered there, letting her captured wrists go when she begged him to, feeling her arms twine around him as he took her nipple in his mouth. She cradled his head, holding him close as he moved to the other breast.

On down he went, biting her lightly right over her rib cage, pressing kisses to either side of her navel, and then moving lower still. He lifted her thighs and guided them over his shoulders.

She kept whispering his name. "Hayes…" All soft and sweet and hungry. "Hayes…"

His name from her lips brought back another flood of memories, the sweetest ones, of the two of them together, young and in love and so certain that nothing could ever break them apart.

They'd trusted each other. *Believed* in each other. She'd sworn never to leave him, and he'd promised the same…

Not that it mattered now. That was the past.

Right now, he had the feel of her, the taste of her, salty-sweet on his tongue. Impossible. And perfect. Right here.

In his arms again.

She caught his head between her hands. Urgently, she whispered his name as he kissed her deeply, using his fingers to bring her closer to the edge. She was so wet, so ready. He stroked her faster.

And then, with a sweet cry, she came. She tossed her head from side to side on the pillow, groaning out his name.

When she settled with a deep sigh, he moved back up her limp body, kissing as he went. Until he reached her lips again and covered them with his own.

She opened for him, kissing him back. And when he raised his head enough to look down at her flushed face and glassy eyes, she said, "I think I'll just lie here, limp and satisfied. Forever."

He smoothed her tangled hair back off her damp forehead. "You are a gorgeous woman. Did I ever tell you that?"

"Often." She grinned, cheeks red, eyes still closed. "You had me convinced I was the most beautiful creature on Earth."

"Because you were—you *are*."

She fake-punched him on the arm. "Or maybe you were just blinded by love."

"Maybe I was. But here we are years later. And you are even more beautiful than before. It's a simple fact. Live with it."

For that, he got a lazy, happy chuckle, one that ended when she reached down between them and took hold of him again. "Oh, my goodness," she whispered. "I mean, honestly…"

"Go ahead. Say it."

"Is this really happening?"

"You'd better believe it." He kissed her. She wrapped one arm around his neck as, below, she continued to drive him wild with that clever stroking hand of hers.

Too quickly, she had him hovering right on the edge. Any second now, he would lose it completely. When he groaned into her mouth, she stroked him faster.

"Hold on, slow down," he pleaded against her parted lips.

"Uh-uh, no way…" She nipped at his lower lip and kept right on driving him out of his mind.

So he took charge, fumbling out a hand for the bed table, getting hold of one of the condoms he'd tossed there.

With another groan, he lifted himself away from her.

"Get back here." She was laughing, a low, teasing sound, reaching for him as he got his knees braced on either side of her and rose up above her. Her eyes, warm amber now, gleamed up at him. "You are a bad, bad man, Hayes Parker." She said it with a wicked little laugh as he rolled the condom down over his aching hardness.

"I do my best." He stared down at her. What a sight. She'd thrown her arms back over her head now. Her hair was spread out on the pillow, a dark, tangled halo around her unforgettable face.

If only he could bottle this moment, store it away, take it out and drink from it on the lonely nights when beauty and softness were nowhere to be found.

She grabbed his shoulders, urging him to cover her.

But he wrapped his arms around her and rolled them, so she was on top. She laughed at that, a joyful sound, and tossed her wild hair. "Really?"

"Really." He clasped the twin inward curves of her waist and lifted her. "Ride me."

"You got it, cowboy."

And then she was straddling him, reaching down, clasping him, guiding him into her soft, wet heat. They groaned in unison as she sank onto him.

"Perfect," he said on a growl. "Come down here," he commanded, reaching for her again to pull her close against his chest.

She resisted, her hair sliding over his throat, feathering along the skin over his collarbones, brushing his cheek as she held his gaze. "Not yet." And she arched her back, bracing her hands behind her on his thighs. She tipped her head to the ceiling. With a breathless little sigh, she started to move.

"Chrissy…" He reached up, cradled those pretty breasts of hers in his two rough hands, feeling the soft weight of them, loving the way her plump, hard nipples pressed into his palms.

"Yes!" she cried. "Oh, Hayes. Yes…" And she kept moving, rocking back and forth on him, making soft, hungry sounds that sent him reeling toward the edge again.

He wanted to go on like this, the two of them, lost in this perfect moment of heat and need and unbearable pleasure. To be swept off forever, just him and Chrissy, connected in this most basic way, free of everyday concerns—about the ranch, about the future they didn't have together, about the tension and hostility his father might bring home with him tomorrow.

Now, in this moment, all the questions somehow seemed answered. He wanted this to last forever.

But then she was tipping her head down to him. He looked up into her dazed, night-dark eyes.

She said, "Now, Hayes. I…can't…"

"Wait," he commanded.

She laughed, the sound slowly morphing into a guttural moan. "Sorry. No can do…"

And then he felt her body closing around him, pulsing in rhythm with the rocking of her hips. She cried his name good and loud then.

He pulled her down to him. She collapsed onto his chest as the finish rolled through her.

That did it. The glorious contraction of her body around him was too much. He lost it.

His climax barreled through him, sweeping everything else into oblivion. There was only the moment, the two of them, together in a way he'd never let himself imagine would ever happen again.

Chapter Nine

Two hours later, Chrissy reached over and turned off the light.

Snuggled close to Hayes in the after-midnight darkness, she traced a slow circle on the bare skin of his chest. "I have news."

"Tell me."

"Well, I had a talk with my insurance guy today."

He caught her hand and kissed her fingertips. "Is everything okay?"

Emotion clogged her throat. "Yeah. It's good news, I promise you."

He lowered her hand to his chest again and gently pressed it flat directly over his heart. She closed her eyes and breathed in carefully through her nose, banishing the tears that threatened to fall.

She was not going to cry. There was nothing to cry about. She and Hayes had just shared an amazing evening in her bed. They had an agreement that this magic between them was just for now.

But really, what was *now*, exactly? They should clarify that.

"So then," Hayes said, his voice a low rumble beneath her palm. "If there's no problem, what did you and your insurance guy talk about?"

"He told me that my insurance will pay for me to rent a room at the inn—or even to rent an apartment if I can find one for just a month or so until my place is live-in ready again. Also, they'll pay your folks for me to stay here."

He frowned. "That's not necess—"

She cut him off with two fingers to his lips. "Don't you dare say it's not necessary. You came back to this town you once swore you'd never set foot in again in order to save this ranch, right? And money to help with that is a good thing, even though it will be a month or two before the check comes through."

He chuckled then. "There never was any arguing with you once you got an idea lodged in that brain of yours."

"I'm right and you know it. Admit it."

"Chrissy—"

"Admit it."

"Fine. You're right. Pay rent if you insist."

"I do insist." She chewed on her bottom lip for a moment. "That is, unless…"

He caught a curl of her hair and slowly wound it around his finger. "What now?"

"Well, I mean, you know…*this*."

"This, what?"

"You and me, Hayes, in bed together again."

He grinned. "Pretty damn spectacular if you ask me."

Those words filled her with giddy, foolish happiness. "You think so?"

"Yes, I do."

"Well, if you're sure…"

"I am."

Her doubts flooded in anyway. She slid her gaze away and asked carefully, "I mean, now that this has happened, maybe you're starting to feel a little…uncomfortable about having me around?"

"Hey."

"Hmm?"

He unraveled the curl of hair he'd wrapped around his finger—and then gave it tug. "Look at me."

She met his eyes. "What?"

"I like having you around."

"You sure? Because now I can afford to go someplace else if you'd rather I—"

"Shh." He cupped the back of her head and pulled her in until their lips could meet in a long kiss that was equal parts tender and playful.

When she lifted her head again, she whispered, "Think about it. Starting tomorrow, your parents will be here. They'll be sleeping in the room downstairs."

"So what? We're not kids anymore. We can sleep where we want to sleep—including with each other. There's a privacy lock on the door to this room and we'll use it." His grin would have made her panties melt right off if she hadn't already shucked them hours ago. "And I'll try not to make you scream too loud."

At that, she gave him a playful slap on the arm. "Rein in that ego, mister."

He cradled her head in his big hand and the look in his eyes turned from teasing to serious. "Stay, Chrissy. Let us have this time together, you and me, for the next few weeks until your place is ready."

No offer had ever sounded quite so tempting. At the same time, she couldn't help wondering how much harder it was going to be to leave him if they spent the next few weeks sharing a bed. "You're sure?"

"Absolutely." He kissed her again, hard and quick this time. "Stay."

Oh, she did want to. But how would she make herself walk away when it was over?

Somehow, she'd have to.

But not for a while yet. In the meantime, why not love every moment for as long as it lasted. "Okay," she replied on a soft husk of breath. "Until my place is ready."

"That's what I wanted to hear." He kissed her again, a hungry kiss that sent heat sizzling through her.

And, well…

Okay, then. So be it. She wanted him and he wanted her and why shouldn't they have this time together?

No, it wouldn't last. He'd made that painfully clear—and so had she, for that matter.

But not everything lasted. Not their young love all those years ago. Not her marriage to Sam, nor his to poor Anna.

Chrissy was old enough now to see the value of living joyfully in the moment. She needed to stop worrying about the future. It would come soon enough. Nothing she could do would stop it.

As for now, though, she would love every minute and not let herself dwell on what would happen when it ended.

In the morning after breakfast, Chrissy called Marisa and then Ruby to invite them to Lionel's welcome-home bar-becue on Sunday. Marisa was out of town, so she couldn't make it. Ruby said she and her four-year-old daughter, Emery, would be there.

Next, Chrissy called her mom. Patrice said yes imme-diately.

Chrissy wasn't surprised. Her mom had never been shy. Patrice liked to be in the thick of things. And an afternoon at the Parker place would include checking in with Hayes's parents and getting a good look at whatever might be going on between Chrissy and Hayes.

"Sweetheart, a party for Lionel," her mother cooed. "What a lovely idea. Of course we'll be there! What shall I bring?"

There was absolutely no need for her bring a single thing. But Chrissy knew better than to say that out loud. Arriving empty-handed would never fly with Patrice Hastings. "How about that broccoli salad you make?"

"Done. And a dessert, I think. I'll make my famous lemon lush."

"Perfect, Mom. See you around two."

As Chrissy ended the call, Hayes came up behind her and wrapped his arms around her. She indulged herself by leaning back against him. "My mom and dad are coming."

"Good." He kissed the word onto the side of her neck. "Austin, Beck and Jake are coming. My sister and Shep, too. I called my mom. She's planning the menu."

"Of course she is."

He dropped another kiss at the spot where her neck met her shoulder. "Arlen said yes, too."

She stiffened. Had she and Hayes just been putting on a show? "Where is he?"

"Relax. He left for the barn a few minutes ago."

She turned her head to look back at him. "We should keep a rein on the PDAs when other people are around."

"Whatever you say." He captured her lips then. It felt so good, his arms around her, his warm mouth moving on hers, his morning beard a little scratchy in a truly sexy way.

She turned in his embrace and slid her eager hands up to wrap around his neck as he caressed his way down her lower back, pulling her in nice and tight so she could feel how glad he was to have her in his arms.

"I should get going," he said softly against her parted lips. "We've got work that needs doing before my dad gets home."

"Okay." She tried to pull away.

He grabbed her tighter. "What I mean is, we're going to need to be quick."

She laughed as he took her hand and pulled her toward the stairs.

At a little before one that afternoon, Norma's Suburban pulled to a stop by the front gate. Lionel was at the wheel.

Hayes had returned to the house a little while before, to be there for his dad's arrival. Chrissy went out the front door and down the walk with him to welcome his dad home and to help carry luggage into the house.

"Don't make a fuss," Lionel commanded when Hayes pulled open the driver's door. "I'm not a damn invalid. I'm feeling fine, and I drove us back from Bronco myself."

Hayes just smiled and clapped his dad on the shoulder. Because it was easy to smile. Didn't matter what raft of crap Lionel piled on his head, Hayes would be alone with Chrissy later and that made everything A-okay with him. "Welcome home, Dad."

"Humph." Lionel got out of the vehicle. "Well, I admit it's good to be out of the hospital and back where I belong." The old man's face softened. He aimed a smile over Hayes's shoulder. "Chrissy Hastings! I heard you've been helping out around the place."

"Lionel." Chrissy stepped around Hayes. "So good to see you."

Hayes's dad gave her a quick hug and then announced, "Let's get everything inside."

By then, Hayes's mom had come around the front of the car to join them. "Go on in," she said to Lionel.

"But I want—"

"We'll bring the stuff in. No problem."

Chrissy stepped up and took Lionel's arm. "This way."

Lionel huffed a little, but he let her lead him along the walk and up the front steps.

Hayes and his mom carried stuff in from the Suburban. When they went in the front door, Lionel was sitting in his recliner, remote in hand, watching *Air Disasters* on the Smithsonian Channel. Rayna sat on the floor beside him, watching him, looking hopeful. As Hayes watched, Lionel reached over and scratched the dog on the head. Rayna gave a happy little whine and braced her nose on the chair arm.

Lionel spotted Hayes. "Beautiful dog," he said. "Well-behaved, too."

Hayes nodded. "She was Anna's."

His dad blinked. "Anna. Your wife…"

"That's right."

"I…"

Hayes smiled, remembering. "Anna had a magic touch with dogs. Horses, too."

"Ah. Well. I'm…sorry, son. I regret that I never met her, and that you lost her." For Lionel, that was a major testimonial.

Hayes felt an ache under his breastbone. "I appreciate that, Dad."

His father clearly had no idea what the hell to say next. But then the door opened again, and his mom came in carrying a small bag in either hand.

"Stay put," she commanded before Lionel could push himself out of the chair. "Hayes and I are managing just fine."

"But I can—"

"Don't," she said sternly. And then, more gently, "Lionel. Relax. Your job right now is to take things nice and easy."

Reluctantly, Lionel settled back into his big chair and returned his attention to the early-model flat screen above the mantel. Hayes carried the bags he'd brought in on through to the downstairs bedroom, and helped his mom put everything away.

"I need to go talk to Chrissy," Norma said once the bags were emptied.

Should he be alarmed? "About what?"

Norma reached up and patted his shoulder. "Shopping. There's lots to do to get ready for tomorrow."

"Right…" He needed to chill. His mom respected boundaries. No way would she be sticking her nose into what might or might not be going on between him and the woman he used to love all those years and years ago.

Norma trotted off to find Chrissy. A few minutes later, the two appeared in the great room together.

"Chrissy and I are headed for the market," his mom said. "There are just a few things we really can't do without for the barbecue tomorrow."

Hayes shut the front door behind the two women and turned back to the great room. His dad was fast asleep in the recliner, with Rayna snoozing on the floor by his chair. The dog didn't even look up when Hayes headed out to find Arlen.

Housed on the bottom floor of a century-old two-story brick building, Tenacity Grocery had rooms to rent on the top floor. Benches lined the wooden sidewalk in front of the store, providing seating for locals to gather and watch the world go by. Rough wooden signs dangled from the long second-floor balcony. The signs announced Beer! Ice! Wine!

Inside the store, the worn wooden floor was slightly uneven. The narrow aisles offered shelves tightly packed with canned goods and other staples. Glass-fronted refrigerators ranged along the back wall. There was a meat counter stuck in the rear corner and two old-fashioned cash registers up front.

Norma grabbed a cart. Chrissy pushed it while Norma loaded it with the items they needed. Walking side by side, they paused as they shopped, taking their time to smile and greet people they knew.

"What do you think?" asked Norma. "More beer, a six-pack of Pepsi and one of Mountain Dew—does your mom still drink Mountain Dew?"

"At a summer barbecue? Oh, you bet."

Norma slipped her arm in the crook of Chrissy's elbow and leaned in close. "I have to say," she whispered. "Just between us girls, it is wonderful to have you staying at the ranch. Reminds me of the old days when you spent almost as much time with us as you did at home. Sometimes lately I do have my fantasies that you and Hayes might—"

"Norma," Chrissy chided fondly. "I'm very grateful to Hayes for offering me a place to stay when I really needed one. That's all it is, though," she shamelessly lied. "Hayes is helping me out."

Hayes's mom clutched Chrissy's arm a little tighter. "Well, I can't help hoping it might turn into more."

You're not the only one, she couldn't stop herself from thinking. But somehow she managed to keep those dangerous words from slipping past her lips.

Really, what was happening to her?

She'd known from the first that Hayes was just being kind, letting her stay here when she needed a place. That they'd ended up in bed together, well, it was a bonus for certain.

But it was never going to turn into love ever after. Hayes had made that way more than clear.

Too bad her hopeless heart wouldn't stop making other plans.

"I need my happy fantasies," Norma said with real conviction. "No matter how tough things get, I'll never change. I'm a shameless romantic at heart."

"Still reading those juicy romance novels?" Chrissy remembered that Norma had always loved a good love story.

"Of course. Love makes the world a better place. In real life *and* in my fantasies. Now come on. Let's get this stuff rung up and get home. We need to get cooking. Tomorrow will be here before we know it."

It was almost ten that night when Hayes tapped on her bedroom door.

Chrissy was feeling kind of contrary by then. Because she'd been lying there for half an hour pretending to read one of Norma's dog-eared paperback love stories, wishing he would come.

Was she pitiful? A lost cause? Oh, yeah.

If she had any sense, she would just stay right there in her bed and not make a peep. Eventually, he would give up and tiptoe back down the hall.

But then he tapped on the door again. And she threw back the covers, leapt from the bed and darted over there.

Pulling the door open a fraction of an inch, she asked, "Who is it?" in a whisper.

"Cute," he said darkly. "Sorry it took me so long. My dad wanted to talk about how I shouldn't have paid any of the overdue bills, hired Arlen or put a new roof on the barn."

She continued to peek through the crack in the door. "Be

nice to your dad. He's still recovering. He's a proud man who hates to show any sign of weakness."

"I *am* nice. Let me in."

"Do you have the secret password?"

Through the crack, she could see him trying not to roll his eyes. "Yeah," he replied. "Let. Me. In."

"Hmm. I'm not sure that's the one."

He seemed unable to decide between smirking at her and scowling. "If you don't let me in, I won't be able to kiss you. Or take off that big shirt you're wearing. Or lay you down on the bed and—"

"Okay!" She pulled the door wide and grabbed his arm. "Password or not, you'd better get in here."

Once she had him over the threshold, she shut the door and turned the lock. Then she stepped in close to him, lifted her arms to rest them on his hard shoulders and got right up in his handsome face. "Get after it, cowboy."

"Yes, ma'am." His mouth swooped down to capture hers as he dipped enough to get those big, rough hands wrapped around the back of her thighs.

She jumped up and hitched her legs around his waist. He groaned against her lips, deepening their perfect kiss as he carried her to the bed.

When he laid her down, he caught the hem of her shirt and whipped it right off over her head. And then he was kissing her as she undid his belt, unzipped his zipper and pushed at his jeans and underwear.

He caught her hands in one of his and held them up over her head as he dug in a pocket and pulled out three condoms. He dropped two on the bed table.

The third, he ripped open. She wiggled her hands free of his grip and helped, pushing his jeans and briefs down far enough that he popped free, all ready to go. He rolled the condom on, eased a finger under the elastic of her panties just enough to get them out of his way.

And then he braced above her on one hand. She stared up into those beautiful eyes of his as he guided himself into her.

It was perfect. Urgent and needful. She cried out at the joy of it, of him, of the two of them, joined. Lifting her legs, hooking her ankles at the small of his back, she surged up until he filled her all the way.

After that, her mind was nothing but a spinning haze of light and wonder. Not caring who might hear her, she cried out his name.

His mouth came down to claim her lips. After that, she was quieter as they moved together, seeking that moment when the gathering heat burst wide open into the sweet, hot pulse of fulfillment.

Hayes woke cradling Chrissy in his arms. It was after five on Sunday morning.

"I'm late," he grumbled, nuzzling her hair.

She laughed, the sound sleepy and way too damn sexy. "Hey!" She tried to grab for him as he slid from the bed. "Where're you going? Get back here…"

"Can't. Arlen's got to be wondering what my problem is."

"Tell him it's all my fault." She propped her head on her hand. Grinning, she watched him as he ran around the room grabbing his clothes. And then she threw back the covers. Without a stitch on, she sashayed up close.

Wrapping those soft arms around his neck, she kissed him. Now he had his mouth on hers and his hands on her body.

Big mistake. Because he really didn't want to go. He deepened the kiss with a low groan.

And she chose that moment to get tough. Clucking her

tongue, she pushed him away and pulled open the door. "Out you go."

"You are a heartless woman."

Standing there in front of him, wearing nothing but a wicked grin, she swept out an arm toward the empty hallway. "Move it."

Grabbing her close, he stole one more kiss before he made himself turn and head off down the hall.

In the barn, he found Arlen mucking out stalls.

Glancing up, Arlen muttered, "You're running a little late, lover boy." He braced his broom against the barn wall and clapped Hayes on the shoulder. "As you can see, I'm almost done with this dirty mess. It's your turn to gather the eggs."

Hayes didn't even argue. How could he? He should have been up an hour ago. Off he went to the chicken coop and those ornery hens with their tendency to peck.

Later, at breakfast, his mom and Chrissy chattered away about their preparations for the barbecue that afternoon as the men shoveled in their eggs and sausage. His dad was pretty quiet. Hayes had no idea what might be going on in Lionel's head. Overall, since his return home yesterday, the old man had been mostly in good spirits. Even last night, when Lionel gave Hayes a hard time for putting his own money into keeping the ranch afloat, the old man hadn't blown up.

But Hayes still didn't trust him to keep his temper in check indefinitely. For way too many years, Lionel Parker had been a bomb looking for any excuse to detonate.

The day turned out to be cooler than usual, and cloudy, but with no rain in the forecast.

For the welcome-home party, Hayes's mom and Chrissy had decided to keep things simple—steaks and burgers with lots of sides. Everybody came who said they would, and they all brought something.

They gathered under a pair of sycamores out in back. Arlen and Hayes had brought out one of the long farm tables from the storage shed. Chrissy and his mom had covered it and two picnic tables with bright checked tablecloths. There were the usual coolers full of beer and soda.

Lionel manned the grill. He wouldn't have it any other way.

Chrissy's mom and dad showed up early. Patrice had brought a big broccoli salad and a huge Tupperware container full of that addictive lemon shortbread and whipped cream dessert she used to serve now and then back when Hayes and Chrissy were a couple—lemon lush. That was the name of it. Hayes had loved that stuff.

Really, it was a great afternoon. Chrissy's friend from the inn, Ruby, had brought her little girl, Emery. The four-year-old was bright and curious.

She hung around by the grill for a bit, asking his dad an endless chain of questions. "Mr. Parker, you look kind of tired. Are you tired?"

"A little, maybe."

"Why don't you take a nap?"

"Well, young lady, I have these burgers to flip and these steaks to keep an eye on."

"Sometimes my mommy tells me a story to help me go to sleep. Do you like stories?"

"Emery, I love stories."

"Good. When you want to take a nap, I will tell you a story."

"Fair enough."

"Can I help you flip the burgers?"

Hayes's dad launched into an explanation of how flipping

burgers was a one-man job. Really, Lionel seemed more than okay with fielding Emery's never-ending questions. But the old man had always been patient with little kids. It was when they got older and stood up to him that the trouble started.

Not that Hayes was bitter or anything…

Jake, Beck and Austin were gathered around the coolers, along with Arlen. Hayes wandered over there and shot the breeze for a bit. Then he sought out his sister and her fiancé, Shep. Rylee seemed so happy. She only looked worried when her gaze strayed toward their dad.

Leaning close to Hayes, she asked, "How's Dad doing?"

He glanced at the grill where Emery was still beaming up at Lionel, chattering away. "Better, I think. He's weak, physically, but he's improving."

"I'm so glad—I mean, that he really does seem to be getting better. It was touch and go there for a while."

"Yeah. He's still stubborn as ever, pushing to take on more than he's ready for. But he and I haven't come to blows yet. So, you know. It's all good."

When they sat down to eat a little while later, Hayes made sure he had Chrissy seated next to him. Wouldn't you know, Patrice and Mel Hastings ended up sitting directly across from them? Mel was his usual friendly, good-natured self.

Hayes braced for attitude from Chrissy's mom. Not that Patrice had ever been awful to him, exactly. She was much too polite for that. But back in the old days, the woman had been certain that her precious only child could do better than Tenacity's best-known bad boy—and she'd had her own subtle ways of making her opinion known. However, she'd softened toward him eventually. By the time he and Chrissy were in their junior year, Patrice had been downright friendly toward him.

But then he and Chrissy had broken up. He'd assumed that Patrice would not be a fan of his now.

Patrice surprised him. She chatted and smiled a lot. And when he finished his burger, broccoli salad, baked beans and fried pickles, she blasted him with a giant smile. "I hope you'll have some lemon lush, Hayes. As I recall you used to love it. And I confess, I thought of you when I decided to make it for today."

He took a moment to come to grips with that. Patrice Hastings had made her famous lemon lush with him in mind? Pigs were flying and hell had clearly frozen right over. "I, uh…yeah, Mrs. Hastings. Of course I'm going to have a giant helping of your lemon lush. I've been looking forward to it since I saw you'd brought it."

"Excellent." Her eyes, the same color as Chrissy's, actually seemed to be twinkling. "And we're all adults now. Please. Call me Patrice."

"Yes. I will. Patrice…"

"Much better. Thank you."

Under the table, Chrissy's hand settled on his thigh, her fingers squeezing a little. He slanted her a warning glance. Because that squeeze had better be just for reassurance. The last thing he needed was Chrissy getting naughty under the table with her mom and dad sitting directly across from them.

Chrissy bumped his arm with her shoulder. He took the hint reluctantly and looked right at her. She gave him her sweetest, most innocent smile.

He wasn't fooled. Everyone considered her such a good girl, an excellent student, a hard worker, big-hearted, helpful and kind. Chrissy was all those things. And she also had a wild streak that he loved a whole hell of a lot. But not right now with Patrice beaming at them from the other side of the table.

Ten minutes later, Hayes's dad got up and made a little speech. "It's been a great day and I have all of you to thank for it," Lionel said in a voice weighted with equal parts fatigue and emotion. "I want you all to know how much I appreciate your coming over to wish me well. I would love to hang around out here till midnight with you. But I'm feeling just a little tired now, so I think I'll head on back to the house." Raising his Solo cup of Diet Pepsi high, he toasted, "Here's to you—all of you!"

A chorus of, "To *you*, Lionel," went up from the group.

After the toast, Ruby McKinley's little daughter ran over to Lionel. He bent down and they shared a few words. The little girl lifted her arms. He bent even lower, and she gave him a hug before running back to sit with her mom.

Hayes stared at his father, thinking of all the years he'd spent on other ranches, chasing a life he could call his own.

And yet somehow, here he was. Back where he started, driven to save the home he'd been so sure he'd left behind forever.

He still felt some bitterness toward his father. But it wasn't the burning, angry kind. Not anymore. Now he watched his mother walk his father back to the house and thought that he still loved the old fool, and that it would hurt really bad to lose him.

But they wouldn't lose him. Not now. Not for a long time, not till years from now. Decades. Because Lionel was recovering and taking better care of himself. He would be fine.

Chrissy touched his arm. "You okay?" she whispered.

He looked down into those big brown eyes and never wanted to look anywhere else.

But he knew that was wishing for the moon.

She would go back to her condo, and he would go…

He wasn't sure where yet. But off to make a life of his own. Once he had everything in order here, once his dad was back on his feet and could run the ranch again, Hayes would be packing up and hitting the road.

Yeah, the money he was spending to keep the ranch going would put a big dent in his plans to buy his own place.

But he couldn't think about all that now—or about how, without his continued hard work and backing, his dad and mom would have a hell of a time staying on top of things here.

It would all work out.

Somehow.

He just needed to keep his eyes on the prize here, keep doing everything he could to get the ranch back in the black. He needed *not* to think about walking away till the time for leaving came.

And even more than that, he needed not to think about losing Chrissy again—because after all, he didn't have her. Not really. What they shared was just for now.

And a man couldn't lose what he didn't have.

Chapter Ten

Chrissy kind of hated to see the party end.

But the next day was a work day, so everyone called it a night around the time it got dark. Rylee and Shep headed back to Bronco. Ruby took her sleepy little daughter home to bed. Hayes's buddies stayed long enough to help put stuff away. Then they drove off, too.

Chrissy, Hayes, Arlen and Norma spent about an hour in the house, washing pots and serving dishes, just generally tidying up.

"What a perfect day," Norma said as she hung up the dishtowel. She circled the kitchen hugging Arlen, Hayes and then Chrissy. "Thank you," she said, "all three of you. Lionel can be tough to deal with, I know. But he loved every minute of the party today. Thank you for making it happen."

She wiped a tear from the corner of her eye and went off to join Lionel in the big downstairs bedroom. Arlen headed for his trailer a few minutes later.

That left Chrissy and Hayes in the kitchen. Just the two of them, alone.

He came up behind her as she went on tiptoe to put a stack of nesting bowls back in the upper cupboard next to the sink. When he grasped her waist with those strong hands of his, she almost dropped the bowls.

"Watch it," she warned, sliding the bowls onto the shelf, then shutting the cabinet door.

"I can't help myself," he whispered, so close now that she could feel the heat of him at her back. His hands glided upward and then inward to cradle her breasts over her shirt and bra. "You're just too damn beautiful to resist."

She laughed, the sound low and husky to her own ears. "No PDAs, remember?" she chided. He felt so good at her back, so strong and solid. His arousal pushed at her through the layers of their clothing. She couldn't wait to get upstairs, couldn't wait to have him naked in her bed.

He let go of one breast to brush her hair out of his way so he could press a line of kisses down the side of her throat. "It's just you and me here in this kitchen—and Rayna." The big dog had made herself comfortable under the table. At the sound of her name, she wagged her tail. It thumped against the wood floor. "Rayna doesn't judge." He scraped his teeth along the path his lips had made. It felt so good, like he'd struck a trail of hot sparks down the surface of her skin.

"Hayes…" Her breath had mysteriously fled her lungs. She sucked in a gasp. "Your mom could—"

"She won't. Relax."

"We should—"

"Shh. Kiss me." He caught her chin, guiding her face around so that he could take her mouth. His lips touched hers and she couldn't resist. She turned in his hold and slid her arms up his chest to twine around his neck.

The world spun away. Hayes filled all her senses. She breathed him in, surrendering completely to the spell only he could cast.

Right now, with her arms around him, her mouth fused to his and her body melting under his touch, she couldn't imagine any other life than one spent with him.

All these years she'd been telling herself that she'd moved on, she'd forgotten him. That he was just a boy she'd loved when they were both too young to know what love really meant.

Wrong. She hadn't moved on. Not really. He was always there, in her heart. She had married Sam, known fresh heartbreak, got divorced and moved back home.

And all that time she'd believed her own lie that Hayes Parker was just a boy she'd loved in high school. It was a lie she could have gone on believing. Maybe for the rest of her life.

If only he hadn't come back. If only she hadn't taken him up on his offer to live here on the ranch with him.

If only she hadn't let him into her bed.

If only…

Too late. Here they were, holding on tight, kissing in the kitchen after dark on Sunday night.

She pulled away.

"Chrissy, wait…" He tried to pull her back to him.

She caught his hand. "Come on," she whispered. "Turn off the light. Let's go to bed."

He didn't argue after that. She led him up the stairs, Rayna following behind.

In her room, he took off all her clothes and then made short work of his. Outside, the clouds had cleared. The moon shone in the window, bathing their bodies in a silvery glow.

It was beautiful, just Chrissy and Hayes, holding each other in the moonlight. Whatever happened later, so be it.

Pushing all her thoughts of the future aside, she gave herself up to right now.

Tuesday morning, Ruby suggested they get lunch together. "The barbecue Sunday was great," Ruby said, her smile bright and sunny as ever, her blond hair catching the light from the lobby fixtures above. "But a little girls-only time never hurts. I'm free at noon if you can get away then?"

"I'm in. The Silver Spur Café?"

"That works."

At noon, they walked over to the café together and got a two-top by the window in front. Their server was quick. In no time, she bustled over with grilled cheese sandwiches and tall iced teas.

They dug right in.

"It's just what I needed," said Ruby. "Melted cheese and grilled bread. Sometimes you can't beat the classics."

Chrissy had her mouth full, but she nodded in enthusiastic agreement.

"So…" Ruby let the word trail off and pitched her voice low, just between the two of them. "You and Hayes Parker…?"

Chrissy swallowed too fast and almost choked. Carefully, she sipped her tea. "Is it that obvious?"

"Well, there's definitely a certain…vibe."

Chrissy laughed at that. "A vibe. There's a vibe…"

Ruby wasn't put off. "Just answer the question."

"Okay, okay. We had a thing, Hayes and me, way back in high school."

"Ah…"

"We were even prom king and queen our senior year, believe it or not."

"Oh, I can picture it now…"

Chrissy faked a giant sigh—one that turned out to be not quite as fake as she'd intended. "But sadly, it didn't work out with Hayes and me."

Ruby wasn't falling for Chrissy's act. She asked seriously, "Did Hayes Parker break your heart?"

Chrissy shrugged and quit trying to play it off. "He did, yeah. He broke my heart, and I broke his and we were finished. Or so I thought for the past fifteen years. Until he came back to town to save the family ranch and…well, stuff happened."

"I have to say," Ruby spoke gently, "judging only from what I saw Sunday, you two seem good together."

Chrissy just smiled. She liked Ruby a lot, but she didn't really want to get down in the weeds about where it was going—or not going—with Hayes. Because she had no idea how it would all turn out and she wasn't ready. Not to lose him. Not to step up and beg him to stay.

When the silence between her and Ruby had gone on too long, Chrissy spoke up, changing the subject. "Your little girl is such a sweetheart. She was adorable with Lionel on Sunday. He can be such a Grumpy Gus. Emery sweetened him right up, though."

Ruby's smile couldn't completely mask the sadness in her eyes. "Emery's my whole life. But sometimes…" She seemed not to know what to say next. Chrissy kept quiet, not interrupting, not pushing her either. Finally, Ruby continued, "Owen and I have been divorced for a year now. Sometimes it seems like forever."

"You miss him?"

"No!" Ruby looked horrified. "My marriage is truly over. I honestly don't want Owen back again. It's just that sometimes I feel guilty that Emery's an only child. That she won't have a little brother or sister, you know?"

Chrissy reached across the small table to run a hand down Ruby's arm. "Seeing you with her the other day, watching her make friends with Lionel, of all people… Ruby, it's obvious you're a great mom and that your daughter is happy. And even if I hadn't seen you with her, just the way you treat the guests at the inn, like each one of them is special, says a lot about who you are. It tells me that you're kind and you care and that your little girl will grow up confident and ready to take on the world."

Ruby grinned. "So then, I take it you think I'm doing all right?"

"I know you are."

"Thank you." Ruby said that with feeling.

"It's only the truth." Chrissy sighed. "I want kids, too. So much. But who knows if that will ever happen."

Ruby was silent, her blue eyes full of understanding. Chrissy had mentioned in the past that her marriage hadn't worked out, so Ruby knew a little about Sam and about the divorce.

"Go ahead." Chrissy held Ruby's gaze. "Whatever you're thinking, Ruby, just say it."

"Well, I did hear that you'd struggled with infertility."

Chrissy sat back in her chair. "I'm not even going to ask who told you that. This is Tenacity, after all. Everybody knows way too much about everybody else."

Ruby's cheeks had turned bright red. "I shouldn't have said anything."

Chrissy touched her arm again. "It's okay. In fact, it's good." She tried to decide how much to say. "I mean, it's a small town. People talk. I consider you a friend and I would appreciate it if you would just tell me what people say about me."

"You're sure?"

"Absolutely."

"Well. Good, then." Ruby drew herself up straighter in the bentwood chair. "And I hope you'll do the same for me."

"It's a deal." Chrissy picked up her iced tea and offered a toast. "To honesty between friends."

"To honesty." Ruby tapped her glass to Chrissy's.

Now Chrissy felt a little guilty. They'd just toasted to honesty, and yet she was only going to say so much. She gave her friend the short version of what she'd told Hayes two weeks before. "Sam's a good man, and a completely conventional sort of guy. He wanted a stay-at-home wife, and he wanted us to have children—as many as possible—together. When we found out that was not going to happen, Sam couldn't deal with it. He wouldn't even try. Our marriage was collateral damage. It was horrible, for me and for Sam. And it was so hard, walking away from our life together."

"Oh, Chrissy." Ruby shook her head. "I'm so sorry. And as far as walking away from your marriage, I know exactly what you mean."

They were quiet for a minute or two.

Then Chrissy said, "I'm so glad you have Emery—and that she has you."

"Yeah." Ruby's beautiful smile bloomed wide. "Me too."

A little while later, they walked back to the inn together. As they went in the side entrance, Chrissy's cell rang.

She checked the display. It was her mom. She didn't have time for a chat right then, so she sent it to voicemail.

On her afternoon break she called her mom back.

Patrice gushed. "We had such a good time Sunday, sweetheart. Thank you for inviting us."

"I'm glad you could come." Chrissy realized as she said the words that she meant them sincerely.

Her mom said, "I have to tell you…"

Chrissy braced herself. "What, Mom?"

"Well, everyone in town is talking about Hayes."

Chrissy stiffened. "What about him?"

"Sweetheart, please. Don't be defensive."

"Well, Mom. Since he came back to town Hayes has

been good to me, and I don't want to hear whatever mean things people are—"

"Wait! Stop. There are no mean things. I promise you, it's good! It's all good."

Surely she hadn't heard right. "Uh, it is?"

"Yes, yes. Everyone's saying what a beautiful thing he's doing, the way he's stepped right up to save the family ranch. Honest and truly, sweetheart, I will always be sad about poor Sam. But the truth is, Hayes has grown up into quite a man—a hero, you might even say."

Chrissy felt humbled. "Yeah. You're right. It's pretty great that he came back now. Lionel and Norma need him so much. And I'm sorry I jumped to conclusions when you said that people are talking about him."

"It's okay. I do understand. When people talk, they're not always saying nice things."

"You're right about that."

"And frankly, I have not always been Hayes Parker's biggest fan. But Hayes has grown into a fine man, sweetheart. And if you two did decide to rekindle that old flame—"

"Mom."

"Hmm?"

"That's not going to happen." It actually hurt to say those words. Partly because they were a lie. The whole rekindling thing had already happened. But the fire wasn't going to last. And she needed to remember that. She needed to keep firmly in mind that she and Hayes were not a forever kind of thing.

"Never say never," Patrice chirped on a happy little laugh.

"Mom…"

"I know, I know. You're at work and you have to go."

"I'll talk to you soon."

"Love you, sweetie."

"Love you, too, Mom."

Chrissy ended the call feeling simultaneously pleased that her mom could now appreciate Hayes, and sad that her time with Hayes couldn't last. It was really starting to get to her that they would lose each other all over again.

It wasn't supposed to be like this, with her pining for a future she just wasn't going to get. She and Hayes had agreed to share a special time. A time where they could enjoy each other and then say goodbye without either of them getting hurt because…

What had they said to each other? That she wasn't ready for love—and that he never would be.

He seemed to be sticking by what he'd said then, standing firm that love remained in the *never again* category as far as he was concerned.

For her, though, it just wasn't that simple. Maybe she still wasn't ready. But oh, sweet Lord, now she wanted to be.

Had she known this would happen?

Probably. But she'd gone ahead anyway. And she didn't regret that.

She would never regret this summer love affair with Hayes.

But the end wasn't that far away—it never had been. Soon, she would move out. They'd agreed they would be over when she returned to her condo. And then, once Lionel was back on his feet, Hayes would leave town. She would never have a future with him.

And for as long as this love affair lasted, she needed to keep a check on her feelings. She needed *not* to say more than he wanted to hear. It was what it was. She'd faced heartache before, and one way or another, she would survive it again.

That night, he tapped on her door at a little before nine. She set aside her sadness and went to let him in.

He hesitated on the threshold. "I have something I'm kind of needing to talk about," he said.

She took his hand and led him to the bed. They sat down side by side. She reminded herself not to hope that he might be about to say he didn't want to let her go when her condo was ready. "I'm listening."

He shut his eyes and drew in a slow breath. "It's just… Chrissy, I can't shake this feeling that here, on the ranch, is where I'm supposed to be."

Hope started to rise again. She shoved it down. This was not about the two of them and she knew that in her heart.

She asked, "So you're thinking about staying on, working with your dad?"

He winced. "You know, when you say it out loud like that, I can't see it happening, not in real life. We both know my dad."

"Hayes." She gave his fingers a reassuring squeeze. "He's better lately, not so quick to fly off the handle."

"He's not *better* enough—but yeah. I'm thinking about it anyway. I have money saved. And when Anna's dad died he left me a little something. I've already been helping out with the bills around here. But if I put in what I have to make things work here, if I go for it…" He drew a slow breath and let it out hard. "I don't know. I can't decide. For fifteen years I've told myself I could never come back home."

"And yet, here you are…"

"You're right." He gave a humorless laugh. "I said never. And yet I couldn't stay away when the old man really needed me. And right about now, I am completely confused."

"You don't have to decide right this minute. There's time."

"I just don't know."

"And that's okay. The right answer will come to you. Eventually."

"I hope so." He flopped back across the bed, tugging on her hand so that she came with him. For a moment, they were side by side staring up at the ceiling. Then he braced up on an elbow and leaned over her. Trailing his index finger up her arm, he paused to trace the words inked on her skin.

Be Bold. Be True. Be Free.

She should be more of all three of those things. But she wasn't.

And his brushing finger was moving on, his light touch gliding all the way to her shoulder and then under the fall of her hair.

When he cradled the back of her neck, she raised her mouth to him.

He kissed her.

All the questions faded away. She got gloriously lost in right now.

That night? It was perfect. And so was the night after.

And the one after that.

Chrissy tried not to let herself feel blue that time was passing way too quickly. That she couldn't help wanting more than Hayes was willing to give. She tried to stay upbeat, to let herself be happy with each day—and night.

But it wasn't enough. She did want more. More than they'd agreed on, more than the magic they conjured between them at night in her bed.

Be Bold. Be True. Be Free.

Her own tattoo seemed to mock her.

And as each day passed, she felt like a bigger coward than the day before. For not taking a chance. For not laying her heart on the line, not just telling Hayes how she felt, not asking him for what she really wanted.

Friday at the dinner table, Hayes said, "Arlen and I are thinking about heading over to the Grizzly tonight, having a beer or two, shooting some pool."

"Sounds like fun," Norma said.

Lionel huffed. "Don't go gettin' wasted, now. Morning comes damn good and early around here."

"Don't worry, Dad," Hayes said in that patient voice he used when Lionel got overbearing. "I'll keep a lid on it."

Arlen added, "And I'll be there to make sure he behaves himself."

"Hmph," said Lionel, and helped himself to more green beans.

Hayes scoffed. "Right. Arlen will keep an eye on me. Because I'm such a yahoo and all."

"Yeah." Arlen grinned. "A yahoo. That's you."

Chrissy felt hurt and despised herself for it. So he wanted to go out for a beer with his friend. He was in no way obligated to spend every night in her bed.

Even if their nights were numbered and counting down to zero fast.

"Chrissy..."

She glanced up to meet Hayes's green eyes—zap! Like a bolt of lightning straight to her heart, just from looking at the guy. Could she be any more pitiful?

"Come with us," he said, his slow smile just for her.

Happiness poured through her—and for what? Because he'd invited her to tag along?

Was she ridiculous?

Definitely.

Ridiculous and lying to herself and miserable—and totally and completely in love.

With Hayes.

All over again.

Her throat locked up with sheer misery. Because she'd gone and done it, admitted it to herself.

She loved Hayes.

And she wished with all her yearning heart that she didn't.

"Chrissy?" He was watching her. She could see the confusion on his face. He had no idea what was going on inside her.

Too bad. They had an agreement, and she was sticking with it. The last thing he ever needed to know was how she'd gone and fallen for him a second time.

And as for tagging along with them to the saloon? Forget it. The Grizzly was the last place she wanted to be right now. "Thanks for thinking of me. But I'm kind of tired. I'm just going to hang around here tonight."

Twin lines formed between his eyebrows. She read his expression. He could see that something was going on with her, but he didn't know what.

And he would never know. He'd made his position painfully clear. It would do neither of them one bit of good for her to go declaring her undying love to him.

She just needed a little time to herself tonight. She needed to start considering what her next move should be.

"You sure?" Hayes asked. He was watching her so intently.

Her heart did something painful inside her chest. For a moment, she just knew he must have read her mind.

But then she realized he was only asking about the visit to the Grizzly tonight.

"Yeah, Hayes. Really. I'm just going to stay here tonight."

He let it go at that and she was grateful. Twenty minutes later, he and Arlen headed for town.

Lionel helped clear the table and then, with Rayna at his heels, Hayes's dad wandered off to his big chair in the great room. Chrissy and Norma cleaned up the kitchen together.

"You're quiet tonight," Norma said as she put the last dish in the dishwasher and started it up.

"Just tired, that's all."

Hayes's mom gave her the strangest look, kind of tender. And also mysterious.

"What?" Chrissy demanded.

The older woman put her hand on Chrissy's shoulder, a warm touch. Reassuring, too. "I do love having you here. I keep hoping you'll stay. You and my son are good together. You always were good together."

Chrissy didn't know whether to argue that point or grab Norma in a tight hug. "Hayes isn't interested in anything serious."

"You sure about that?"

"He told me so. He was real clear on the subject."

"Come here." Norma clasped her other shoulder and pulled Chrissy close. It felt good hugging Hayes's mom. It gave Chrissy comfort, and she needed that right now. Then Norma took her by the arms and held her away. "If he lets you go again, well, I don't know what. That's just wrong and I don't mind saying so."

Chrissy couldn't help laughing—the kind of laugh that hovered on the verge of tears. "And here Hayes and I thought you and Lionel had no idea what was going on upstairs while you were sleeping."

Norma pressed her hand to Chrissy's cheek. "Oh, honey. We didn't get to be this old without learning to mind our own business at least some of the time."

Chrissy laughed again then, and Norma laughed right along with her.

"What's so funny in there?" Lionel called out from the other room.

"I almost dropped a serving bowl!" Norma hollered back.

"Be careful!"

"We will, we will!" Norma put her hand on Chrissy's shoulder again and lowered her voice. "If you haven't told him how you feel, think about it. Honesty really is the best policy."

"Not in this case. He doesn't want to know."

"But maybe *you* need to say it to him."

Chrissy thought about Norma's words as she dried the last saucepan. She climbed the stairs thinking about them.

They ran through her mind as she washed her face and brushed her teeth.

Around nine, when she stood on the rag rug by the bed trying to decide whether to read a book or get a head start on the menus for the week after next, she was still thinking about it.

And still coming to the same conclusion.

Hayes didn't want to know, and she wasn't going to tell him.

Period. End of story.

She was just climbing into bed with a nice, fat novel about two women opening a bookstore at the beach in Malibu, California, when there was a tap on the door.

Her heart rate blasted into overdrive. She ordered it to settle down, reminding herself that it was way too early for Hayes to be home from the bar.

"Chrissy?" He called her name quietly.

Her heart raced even faster. And she couldn't breathe.

Yep. Ridiculous. No doubt about it.

Sucking in air, ordering her pulse to slow the heck down,

she dropped her book on the nightstand and went to let him in.

He stood on the threshold, hands stuffed in his pockets.

"You're back early." Her voice sounded bizarrely normal, though inside she was a riot of warring emotions—panic, dread, misery, excitement...

"I kept thinking about you," he said, "kept wondering what you were up to."

"Well, I'm up to no good, obviously." She tried to sound playful, but the effort fell flat. She was miserable and, at the same time, so glad to see him—like he'd been away forever when in fact he'd been gone, what? A couple of hours? It was just more proof that she'd somehow managed to lose her mind over the man. And for the second time, too. Really, she ought to know better.

He peered at her, frowning. "You feeling okay?"

"Uh. Yeah. Fine. Why?"

"Well, at dinnertime, you said you were tired, that you wanted to take it easy..."

"That's right, I did."

"So I was worried about you."

"Hayes, I told you. I'm fine. Stop worrying."

"It doesn't work that way. You seemed... I don't know, unhappy. Or maybe sick. Are you sure you aren't coming down with a bug?"

"I'm not sick. There's no bug. I keep telling you I'm fine." She hoped he would leave it at that. But he just went on frowning at her, so she added, "It's been a long work week, that's all. A long week with lots going on."

He just stood there and stared at her. Finally, he asked, "Chrissy?"

"Yeah?"

"Do I get to come in?"

She hesitated, yearning for him at the same time as she wished he would just go away. "Uh. Sure. Of course." She stepped back and gestured him forward, shutting the door as soon as he was inside.

And then, all over again, they just stood there staring at each other.

It was excruciating.

And then he closed the short distance between them and took her face between his two hands. "Just tell me what's wrong." He looked a little freaked out. And apparently, he was. Because then he said, "You're scaring me."

She tipped her head back, groaned at the ceiling, and admitted to herself that Norma was right.

Too bad if he didn't want to hear it.

She needed to say it. "Look…"

"Yeah?" Gently, with slow care, he guided a few stray strands of hair away from her eyes.

That sweet touch undid her. She wanted to cry. "Oh, Hayes…"

"What? Tell me. Whatever it is. I'm here. I'm listening."

"I didn't mean for this to happen. I didn't expect it. Not in a hundred years…"

His mouth fell open—and then he seemed to pull himself together. He framed her face between his palms again and whispered, "I know you said there were…issues with Sam. That you never got pregnant. But just tell me. Are you somehow magically pregnant now?"

A weird, ragged laugh burst out of her. "No! Hayes, think about it. We've been careful. Not to mention we've been together that way for what, a week? Even if I was, I wouldn't know at this point."

He kept holding her face. And he looked at her so deeply. "So then, not pregnant?"

"Uh-uh. Not pregnant."

"Well, whatever it is, whatever you need, Chrissy, I'm here for you. I promise you. I want to help with whatever is bothering you."

She caught his wrists and gently peeled his hands away from her face. "I just need for you *not* to be touching me when I tell you. Okay?"

"Uh, sure." He dropped his arms to his sides and fell back a step. "All right. Not touching you. Now what the hell is wrong?"

"I, uh…" Dear Lord, this was awful.

"Come on. You're killing me here."

"I'm sorry. It's just… Oh, Hayes. It's like this. I'm in love with you, okay? I'm in love with you all over again."

His face went blank. He actually fell back another step—like she'd pushed him. Or maybe like he really needed to get as far away from her as possible. "Chrissy, look…" He shook his head.

He actually shook his head.

She closed her eyes and drew a slow, careful breath. This was bad. She'd known it would be. And yet she'd gone and said those dangerous words anyway. "Tell you what, Hayes Parker. Just do it, okay? Just put me out of my misery."

He had the nerve to wince. "Chrissy, I really don't want to—"

"—hurt me?" It came out as an accusation. Because it was one. "You don't want to hurt me?"

He looked downright crushed. "You're right, I don't. I mean that."

She threw up both hands. "Well, too bad. Because you've gone and done it anyway."

He backed up yet another step and demanded in a near-whisper, "Why are you so angry?"

Because you don't love me back! Because you'll never love me back! She wanted to scream at him, just run around the room in circles, screeching like her hair was on fire.

But she couldn't do that. She might be half out of her mind with the awfulness of laying her heart on the line and having him step back in horror and remind her that he didn't sign on for this. But so what? That was her problem. Her pain to deal with.

He *hadn't* asked for this.

In fact, he'd warned her upfront. He'd said it right out, made it perfectly clear that he wasn't going to be falling in love with her, or with anyone. Not ever again.

And she was totally in the wrong to keep torturing both of them this way.

"Chrissy, I—"

"No." Now she was the one putting up both hands and backing away. "You know what? This is my fault. This is me just…humiliating myself."

"No, that's not true. You're not. No way. You're being honest. And listen, I—"

"Stop. I mean it. Please just stop." Her stomach churned and her face felt hot enough to melt right off her bones. "I don't know what I was thinking to lay this on you. It was wrong and I apologize. And, well, that's pretty much it."

He gulped and glanced away as he forked his fingers through his unruly hair. "What are you saying?"

She wanted out. Now. "Well, Hayes, I just think that it's time for me to go."

He blinked at her. "You mean you've suddenly decided that you're moving out?"

She drew herself up. "Yeah. That is exactly what I mean."

"But why? It's not necessary. We can—"

"Hayes. No, we can't. Not unless you can look in my

eyes and tell me that you love me, too—or that at least, given time, you might be able to."

"Oh, Chrissy..." His tone, his sad eyes—they said it all. "Just don't leave, okay? There's no reason for you to leave."

She patted the air between them, as though the gesture could somehow ease the awfulness of what was happening here. "From my point of view, there is every reason for me to leave. I mean, maybe *you* could work it out with me so that you're okay with me and my feelings. But I can't. I am not okay with your feelings about me. I shouldn't have said anything, but I did. I can't call the words back. They're out. You know now. And I hate that. I can't deal with that and also have to see your face every day."

"But—"

"Stop. Listen. I don't want to live in the same house with you anymore. I'm finished here. I need to go, I really do. I'm going to call my dad first thing tomorrow and have him get over here with a truck. I'm hoping to be out before lunch."

There was a gaping hole of silence then. Finally, Hayes asked through gritted teeth, "That's it? You mean it? You're leaving just like that because I won't say I love you?"

"Finally. You're getting it. Yes, Hayes. I love you and you don't love me. It's awkward and it's painful. I want out and you should *want* me to go."

He shook his head. And then, with a slow breath, he faced her squarely. "You know what? Fine. You go ahead. Go." He turned for the door.

She knew she should stop him, that she should at least take a stab at smoothing things over with him. She didn't want it to end like this—as bad as the first time she lost him, in that crappy old trailer down in Wyoming.

But what could she say? There was no way to make it all better.

It was awful and she didn't know what to do about that. Right now, she had neither the will nor the heart to fix anything.

All she wanted was out.

So she did nothing. She stood there with her mouth firmly shut and watched him walk out the door.

Chapter Eleven

At six the next morning, Chrissy called her dad.

He answered on the first ring. When she told him what she wanted, he said, "I can be there at eight with a truck. Will that work?"

"Yes." By eight, she figured Hayes and Arlen would be done with breakfast and back out on the land. "Thank you, Dad. I love you so much."

"I love you, too, Sugar Bee. See you then."

She went down to help Norma with the morning meal. Hayes and Arlen came in at seven. Chrissy smiled a greeting at Arlen and tried not to look at Hayes because looking hurt too much. Lionel and Rayna wandered in from the downstairs bedroom five minutes later.

Somehow, Chrissy got through the meal, putting food in her mouth and chewing it, sipping coffee, trying to force her lips into a smile when anyone spoke to her.

Hayes and his dad got into an argument about when Lionel would be ready to get out and help with chores.

"For God's sake," grumbled Lionel. "It's not going to kill me to gather a few eggs."

Norma didn't want Lionel out working yet either. "Hayes and Arlen are managing just fine," she said, her eyes narrowed on her husband. "I want you to take it easy for at least another week before you try handling any chores."

"It's a walk, Norma. I walk out to the chicken pen, I walk around the coop collecting the eggs and then I walk back here to the house. Walks are good for me. The doctor said so."

Norma shook her head. "You know there's more involved in egg gathering than just walking. I'm not going to argue with you anymore. One more week of taking it easy. That's all I'm asking. Then you and me can go visit the chicken coop together."

Lionel was not pleased. He got up in a huff and headed for his room with Rayna trailing in his wake. A few minutes later, Hayes and Arlen carried their plates to the sink and went back outside to work.

Chrissy's dad was due in about fifteen minutes. She got up and started grabbing stuff off the table to clear it.

Norma said, "All that will wait. Sit down and tell me what's going on."

Chrissy's eyes filled with tears. She blinked them away as she dropped back to her seat. "Oh, Norma…"

Norma slid over to the chair next to Chrissy's. Leaning close, she laid a soothing hand on Chrissy's back. "It's okay, honey…"

"No. No, it's really not."

"Now, now. Sometimes it's better just to let it all out."

"Is it? I don't know about that. I don't even know how much to say. Things just kind of blew up between Hayes and me, and now I need to get away. So I called my dad and he'll be here in a few minutes to move me out."

Norma's mouth formed a shocked O. "Hayes asked you to leave?"

"No. He wants me to stay. But I, um, told him I love him,

and he turned me down and now I really need to go and stay somewhere else."

Norma pulled her closer. "Oh, honey. It's all my fault."

"No…"

"Yes. I talked you into telling him how you feel."

"Norma, no. No, you did not. You said maybe I needed to tell him. I thought about that. And I realized that I did want him to know. So I told him. I took my shot, and it didn't go well. That's what happened. It was my choice to open my big mouth, and this is the result."

"I'm still sorry. And I'm going to miss having you here, honey. I'm going to miss you so much."

"Oh, I'll miss you, too. I really will."

Norma pulled her closer. Chrissy let Hayes's mom hold her, just for a minute or two.

Then, with a sigh, she kissed Norma on the cheek. "Come on, now. Let's clean up this kitchen. And then I need to get started hauling all my stuff down the stairs."

By the time her dad arrived with one of the workers from the store, Chrissy's eyes were dry. With Norma's help they got everything downstairs and out to the truck.

After her dad drove off, Chrissy went in to say good-bye to Lionel.

Hayes's dad looked sad at her news. "You come to visit. Any time. You hear me?"

She thanked him and gave him a quick hug.

Before she got into her Blazer to go, she wrapped her arms around Norma again.

"Don't you dare be a stranger," Hayes's mom whispered.

"Oh, Norma, give me a little time to pull myself together. I'll call you in a week or two. We can meet for coffee or something."

"Yes. Yes, let's do that." Norma hugged her even tighter before she finally let her go.

It was a few minutes after eleven when Chrissy turned into the driveway of her parents' house. Her mom came running out to greet her.

"Chrissy!" Patrice grabbed her in a hug—and then surprised her by not fussing any more than that. They all got to work unloading the clothes and belongings Chrissy would need for the next few weeks. Everything else, her dad and his helper, Tim, took to store in the warehouse with the rest of her furniture and household goods.

The afternoon went by in a blur. She couldn't believe that she was really back in her old room in her parents' house again. She'd tried so hard not to let that happen.

And yet somehow, it had. At least her mom had cleared out all the fluffy pastel bedding and repainted her Pepto-Bismol–colored walls a nice, relaxing pale blue.

Her mom came in as Chrissy finished hanging up her clothes.

"So," Patrice said briskly. "What can I help you with?"

"Thanks, Mom." Chrissy dropped to the side of the bed. "But I've got it handled."

"You sure?"

"Yes—and I want you to know how much I appreciate that you're here for me to come home to."

Her mom walked toward her slowly. "Sweetheart. Are you okay? Is this about Hayes?"

She didn't even have the energy to lie about it. "Yeah."

"I'm so sorry." Her mom whispered the words.

Somehow, her mother's gentle approach had Chrissy reaching out a hand. "I can always use another hug."

"Oh, my baby…" Patrice dropped down beside her. Chrissy hugged her mom close. She breathed in Patrice's flowery scent and let herself be glad to have loving arms around her. "Don't you worry, sweetheart," her mom whispered. "Hayes Parker is a stubborn one. But he will come to his senses. You just need to give that man a lot of leeway and plenty of time to come around."

"Oh, Mom. I don't know about that."

"Well, I do. He's a good man," Patrice said softly as she stroked Chrissy's hair. "He can be difficult, I know. But he does have a good head on his shoulders. And he really does love you, sweetheart. You two were always meant to be together."

Okay, now. That was just more than Chrissy could take without talking back.

She lifted her head off her mom's shoulder and said, "Please. What have you done with my real mother? Suddenly you're Team Hayes? What about Sam? I thought you were waiting for him to come back to me."

Patrice gave a small shrug. "Yes, well, I see things differently now. I'm older and wiser."

Chrissy blinked at that one. "Older and wiser than… last week?"

Patrice waved a hand. "Oh, sweetheart. You never did have the connection with Sam that you share with Hayes. I see that now. I see that Hayes is a good man, too—and of course, he's also a goner."

"A goner?"

"That's right. A goner for you. He's in love with you. It's so clear how he feels. He looks at you like you're the most important thing in the world. Are you trying to tell me that you don't know?"

"Mom. Yes. I'm telling you that I don't know because it isn't true. Hayes isn't—"

"Oh, yes. Yes, he is. It was so obvious last Sunday. That

man can't take his eyes off of you. But as I said, he's also stubborn. And that means he needs a little time to come to grips with the fact that he doesn't want to live without you."

"Mom. Come on. I love you so much, but—"

"And I love you."

"But, Mom, sometimes you just don't know what you're talking about."

Patrice shook a finger at her. "Oh, yes, I do."

"He's not going to be coming after me."

"Oh, yes, he is—and if you're impatient for him to get over whatever's holding him back, there is another option."

Chrissy knew she shouldn't ask. "What option is that?"

"You could go to him to try to talk some sense into him—you know, be bold and true, like it says on your arm. And free, too." Patrice frowned. "Though in this case, maybe not so much free as just bold and true."

Chrissy laughed then. It felt good after all this misery she'd been stewing in since last night. "Oh, Mom..." Chrissy rested her head on her mom's soft shoulder again.

And she tried really hard not to hope that her mom actually knew what she was talking about. She tried not to let herself imagine that any day now Hayes would be knocking on the front door, begging to speak to her, ready to plead with her to give him one more chance to make it right.

All day Saturday, Hayes was deeply indignant that Chrissy had just packed her stuff and left. On top of his simmering fury at her, he also happened to be just plain miserable.

How in holy hell had it turned out like this—with him missing her as much as he had when they broke up the first time?

Not that her leaving this time constituted a breakup.

It didn't. How could they break up? They hadn't even

been together this time—not really. This time they'd agreed it was a just-for-now, friends-with-benefits situation.

You couldn't break up when you weren't even a couple.

Or so he kept reminding his own sorry ass.

He missed her already and she'd only been gone since after breakfast—missed her like a *friend*. Because that's what she was—a friend with benefits. Spectacular benefits.

And it damn sure rankled that she hadn't even stuck around to talk this problem out with him. If she really didn't want him in her bed anymore, well, fair enough. He didn't like it, but he was bound to respect her wishes on that score.

Losing Chrissy as a friend, though. That cut him deep. He'd let himself get way too accustomed to their evenings on the porch, to letting himself imagine that the two of them would always be on each other's side from here on out.

As for her saying that she was in love with him all over again, well, what was he supposed to do with that? He'd told her he wasn't going there. She knew that.

Damn. He wanted to call her, call her and remind her that she was being completely unreasonable. They needed to work this problem out. Because he had no intention of losing her all over again. He wanted her in his life.

And if she *loved* him so much, well, why the hell did she leave?

That night at dinner, he announced that he was heading for the Grizzly again. "I feel like I missed out, coming home early last night. I need to make up for lost time."

Arlen said, "Have fun."

It wasn't the response Hayes had hoped for. "I will. And so will you. Because you know you're coming with me."

"No. Not me. I'm hanging out here tonight."

"Aw, come on. Come with me."

"No. Once a week at the Grizzly is way more than enough for me."

Hayes's dad chose that moment to throw in his two cents worth. "Arlen's right. Two nights in a row at that saloon is two nights more than any man needs."

"Stay out of it," Hayes snarled at his dad.

Lionel huffed out a breath. "I got a right to an opinion at my own kitchen table."

"Okay, then, Dad. You have shared your opinion and I have heard it. Now if you don't mind, this discussion is between Arlen and me."

Arlen rose. "This discussion is over, at least as far as I'm concerned. Norma, legendary meat loaf. Thank you, ma'am."

His mom gave Arlen her sweetest smile. "Arlen, hon, you have a nice night."

With a nod, Arlen picked up his plate and carried it to the sink.

Hayes debated taking another stab at getting his friend to ride over to the Grizzly with him—but never mind. When Arlen dug in his heels, there was no budging him.

So then. Fair enough. He'd go on his own. He needed the distraction. Maybe if he got drunk enough, he could stop being so mad at Chrissy for walking out on him like she had.

His dad was staring right at him. "Don't be a damn fool, son. You're in no condition to go out drinking tonight."

"Condition? I don't have any condition. I don't know what you're talking about."

"Yeah, you do. Don't think you're fooling anybody because you're not. You've got that wild-eyed, looking-for-trouble gleam in your eyes. The one you used to get just before you ended up doing something everyone was going to regret. I thought you'd grown out of that but look at you now. Bad as ever. If you leave this house tonight, you're just going to get yourself into trouble. I know it. Your mom knows it. Arlen knows it."

"I am perfectly fine."

"No, you're not. Stay home."

He opened his mouth to tell his father *again* to mind his own damn business.

But then before he got a word out, his mother piled on. "Stay home, Hayes. Your father's right. Whatever you're looking for tonight, you're not going to find it at the saloon. And the chances are much too high that you'll find trouble instead."

Grabbing his empty plate, he shoved back his chair. "I'm out of here." He carried the plate to the sink, took great effort to set it down quietly—and then headed for the door.

Rayna trailed after him. He turned on her. "Stay," he commanded.

With a worried whine, she dropped to her haunches just as his father called from inside the arch to the kitchen, "Don't be a damn fool!"

Hayes didn't answer. He was already out the door and pulling it shut behind him. In his truck, he gunned the engine and took off toward the gate.

It wasn't till he'd driven about halfway to town that he started feeling like the biggest jerk on the planet.

Probably because he'd been behaving like one.

He pulled over to the shoulder, turned off the engine and punched the dashboard twice. Not too hard, though. By then, he was already cooling off.

Fine then. Chrissy was gone and he needed to start getting used to that. It wasn't the first time. And her leaving was probably for the best. He'd been getting way too attached to her all over again, now hadn't he?

And getting attached wasn't good. Because now he felt like he'd lost her twice.

You'd think at some point, he'd learn his lesson. Getting too attached was a bad, bad idea.

As for the Grizzly, the more he thought about it, the less he wanted to be there tonight. But to hell with turning around and heading straight back home.

He realized now that he didn't want to talk to anyone tonight. So when he started up the truck again, he just drove around, looking at the moon out the windshield, trying not to think at all.

It was well after midnight when he let himself back into the darkened ranch house. Rayna appeared, wagging her giant tail. He bent and lavished attention on her.

In the kitchen, he filled a glass with tap water and drank it down. And then he went up the stairs, Rayna right behind him. Somehow he resisted the temptation to wander on down to the end of the upstairs hall, to stand in the doorway of the bedroom there, staring at the empty space where Chrissy used to be.

In the morning, he was up at four. Arlen met him at the barn.

His friend looked him up and down. "I see you survived the night. Have a good time?"

"I've had better."

Arlen clapped him on the arm. "Come on. Let's get to work."

Work was exactly his plan. He figured it was smarter than drinking. From now on, he'd be up at four and getting stuff done, wearing himself out so when he dropped into bed at night, he'd go out like a light, dead to the world.

No spare down time to sit around and sulk about Chrissy.

No opportunity to start wondering if he'd messed up big-time letting her get away. He had a plan.

And on Sunday, Monday and Tuesday, he executed it.

Too bad the plan was crap. He thought of her all the time, and he needed to stop that. He told himself it was merely a matter of focus, that he just had to keep working, pushing himself constantly, until the day came when he didn't think of her at all, when he was too worn out to lie awake at night longing for the woman he couldn't let himself have.

Wednesday, after breakfast, Hayes and Arlen were headed out to the tractor shed to spend some time repairing machinery when a couple of heifers came wandering toward them down the dirt road that led off toward a far pasture. Wandering heifers pretty much always meant a fence was down, so they grabbed what they'd need to repair the damage, tacked up their horses and drove those heifers back to where they belonged. The whole process, including fence repair, took a few hours.

They got back to the barn around eleven, untacked the horses, put their tools away and were headed to the tractor shed when Hayes's mom came out the back door calling his dad's name. She spotted them and waved them over.

About then, his dad sat up in the tall, dry grass midway between his mom on the back porch and Hayes and Arlen on the way to the shed. "Over here!" Lionel hollered as Rayna, who'd been lying right beside him, stood up and wagged her tail.

Hayes, Arlen and Norma ran toward the old man. His dad shouted, "Settle down, settle down! Nobody died!"

The three converged on him. Lionel was sweating right through his shirt and his face was dead white except for two bright patches of red at his cheeks. Whining her concern, Rayna backed out of the way.

"Lionel!" cried his mom. "What in the world...?"

"I said, settle down," his dad grumbled. "I'm fine, just fine."

"Dad. You don't look fine."

Lionel held up a hand to Hayes. "Quit your yapping and give a man a boost."

"Slow down, Dad. Just rest for a moment more before you—"

"I don't need a rest. I need to get on my feet. Help me up, damn it!"

"Lionel," said his mom in a coaxing tone. That was as far as she got.

His dad snapped, "Norma, don't start!" as he kept right on groping for Hayes's hand.

Resigned, Hayes pulled him up. With a lot of groaning and huffing, Lionel got upright. "Come on," said Hayes. "Let's get you into the house." He wrapped his dad's arm across his shoulders.

Arlen stepped up on the old man's other side and Rayna herded them all from behind as Hayes's mom ran ahead to open the back gate and then the back door.

With Lionel grumbling and panting the whole way, they got him inside to his chair, which he immediately flipped into the reclining position. "Get back." He shooed them off. "Let a man breathe."

"What happened?" Hayes's mom cried.

"Norma, relax. A few chickens got loose. I just went out to get them back inside the pen. They were frisky and they tired me out, so I stretched out in the grass to rest a bit."

"You're sweating and your color's off."

"Leave me be. I'll be fine."

She had her phone in her hand. "I am calling Doctor Bristol." As Lionel kept on griping that he was fine and he was going nowhere, Norma got hold of Dr. Bristol's office in Bronco Heights and spoke to a nurse. As for Hayes and Arlen, they just stood there, waiting to find out if they were going to be loading Lionel into a vehicle and getting him off to Bronco Valley Hospital again.

"Okay, then. Thank you, Emily." Norma hung up and turned on Lionel. "Doctor Bristol's nurse has given strict instructions that I'm to check your vitals and call her right back. If anything is out of whack, off we go to the hospital again."

"Humph. We'll see about that."

Norma turned to Hayes and Arlen. "You boys go pour yourselves some coffee. I just made some fresh. I'll check your father over and then we'll see what happens next."

Ten minutes later, Hayes and Arlen sat on the sofa sipping coffee as Norma called Dr. Bristol's office again and reported Lionel's temperature, pulse rate and blood pressure while the whole time Lionel kept insisting, "I'm fine, I'm fine. I'm not even sweating anymore. Just look at me!"

"All right then," Norma said into the phone after both the nurse and Lionel stopped talking. "Will do." She ended the call and then turned to Hayes's dad. "All right. You're to stay in the house and rest all day, and I will be monitoring you hourly."

"I only wanted to get the damn chickens back in the pen. It's not the end of the world, Norma," the old man insisted.

By then, Hayes had had about enough. He set his mug down hard enough that coffee sloshed out. "Knock it off, Dad. Can't you see she's trying to make sure you're all right?"

"And she could have just asked me, now couldn't she? I've been trying to tell the three of you that there is nothing wrong with me and nobody is listening to me. Pardon me if

I've had about enough of all this fussing and fiddling and freaking out when there's nothing to be freaking out about."

"You had acute pancreatitis and you could have died, Dad. People are worried about you."

"And you can all damn well knock that off. I'll have you know I didn't die. And as for all of you hovering over me, I've had enough. You need to give a man some peace!"

Right then, in the middle of another pointless argument with his dad, Hayes thought of Chrissy—Chrissy packing up and leaving. He stood there with his mouth hanging open, realizing that he'd said all the wrong things and now she wanted nothing to do with him. He'd probably never see her again.

Somehow, he was going to have to accept that she was gone—gone again. And she wasn't coming back.

And just thinking that made something snap inside him.

He stared down at his mule-stubborn father and thought, *Lionel Parker, you can go straight to hell.*

Because Hayes couldn't keep on like this anymore. Yeah, he wanted to save the ranch. But he'd had about enough of his dad constantly taking stupid chances with his health and then bitching and moaning when someone tried to help him.

Lionel was still talking. "You hear me, Hayes? You understand what I'm saying to you?"

"Damn right I do!" Hayes was yelling now, too.

"Don't you shout at me, boy! By God, you'd better tone it down."

"Okay, Dad. Yeah. Good idea. I'll tone it down—while I'm walking out the door." He stepped sideways to escape from behind the coffee table and headed for the stairs.

"Hayes, you get back here!" his father shouted.

His mom wrung her hands. "Oh, Hayes. Come on, now. Settle down. Let's talk about this quietly."

Arlen said nothing. He knew better than to insert himself into the middle of a family fight.

In no time, Hayes was up the stairs and entering his childhood bedroom. It wasn't till he turned to slam the door behind him that he realized Rayna had followed him up there. The minute he spotted her, she dropped her butt to the floor and looked up at him through sad, soulful eyes. A small whimper escaped her.

"Sorry, girl. We're out of here."

With an unhappy whine, she flopped to the floor and put her head on her paws.

Hayes couldn't stand to look at her—at those big brown eyes reproaching him. He spun around and made for the closet, where he grabbed three duffel bags and tossed them on the bed. Then he started pulling things from the bureau and stuffing them in the bags.

He kept thinking of Chrissy, which was pointless. And wrong. But still, he kept wishing...

What?

That things could have been different. That *he'd* been different when she said she loved him.

Because what the hell was wrong with him—to go turning her down? He should have been braver. Should have grabbed her and held on and said, yeah. Let's do this. Let's be together. Let's make the kind of life we used to dream about, you and me.

At the very least, he should have agreed to try.

Because turning her down to save himself from another heartbreak wasn't going so well. Somehow, his heart had gotten broken anyway—the worst kind of broken. The kind he'd caused by his own damn self.

He was stuffing a pile of underwear into one of the duffels when he heard a low, throat-clearing sound from behind him. "Son…"

He dropped the underwear on the bed and turned. "What now?"

"Son, I'm sorry." His dad stood on the threshold, looking worn out, regretful and very determined.

Hayes had to blink really hard—partly to clear the embarrassing moisture from his eyes. And partly because he still couldn't believe what he was seeing. What he was hearing…

"I'm a foolish old man," Lionel said, his voice low, rough as a patch of bad road. "A foolish old man with way too much useless pride. I know it, I truly do. I know it, though it practically kills me to make myself admit it—especially right out loud. And even more so to you…"

"Dad." Hayes got the one word out. But he didn't know what he meant to say next.

Turned out that was okay, because his dad said, "It hurt my pride to have you see me laying out there in the grass, worn out from chasing a few ornery hens, just trying to scrape up enough energy to get back to the house. It hurt my pride, so I did what I always do, turned it back around on you—and on your mother, too. I have already said I'm sorry to her. And being the angel she is, she's accepted my apology right off, though I know I do not deserve that woman. I…well, son. I guess the hard truth is I don't deserve you, either. But I truly am so sorry—though, believe me, I know that being sorry is not enough. I know I've got to do better. But to start, let me just say what I should have said weeks ago, on the day you came home again.

"Hayes, thank you. Thank you for coming home—and please. Don't go. This land is yours as much as it ever was mine. Your mother said she told you that I never did disinherit you. She says you know now that that was a mean, ugly lie."

"Yeah, Dad. She told me the truth a while back."

Lionel hung his head. He was breathing heavy.

Hayes went to him. "You should sit down." His dad didn't even argue. He let Hayes lead him to the bedside chair and help down into it. Hayes hovered close. "You need anything?"

His dad looked up at him. "If you would sit, hear me out...?"

"Okay." Hayes went to the bed, shoved the duffels off on the far side, and sat down. "Okay, what? Talk."

Lionel drew a slow breath. "I, uh, I got a bad habit of saying things I shouldn't, things that make me a hard man to forgive. I got too much pride and not enough self-restraint. I'm going to work on that—and no, I don't expect you to believe me." He straightened his slumped shoulders and looked squarely at Hayes then. "But I do want to ask you, please, to stay. Let this time be different. This time don't allow me to drive you away. Because I need your help. I truly do. I need your help bad. Son, do you think that maybe you might see your way clear to sticking around, after all?"

Hayes studied his dad's roadmap of a face. "All right. I'll tell you the truth. I don't want to go. I've tried for years to convince myself that I've moved on. But it was a lie. The plain fact is, I love this ranch. I want to make this place everything we both know it could be."

"Hell, yes!" said Lionel. "I want that, too."

"But Dad. You really pissed me off just now."

Lionel let out a hard breath. His big shoulders slumped. "I get it. I was a jackass, worse even than usual. There was just something so embarrassing about those damn chickens running loose, pecking and clucking, moving too fast for me to catch."

Hayes nodded. "Yeah, I can see how that might get you riled up—and Dad, listen. I was no prince just now either. I lost my temper, too. And not just because you were out of line. For a few days now, I've been having this powerful urge…"

His dad asked gently, "What kind of urge?"

"The urge to run away from my own mistakes."

His father understood. "You mean Chrissy, don't you?" Seeing the understanding in his dad's eyes really got to him. Hayes glanced away. Lionel said, "I miss having her around, I truly do. And I've got to tell you, that one's a keeper."

Hayes hung his head. "Yeah. She is."

"Don't make the same mistake I did. Don't drive the ones you love away."

Hayes didn't know what to say. He muttered, "Too late, Dad. I already did. I messed it up with her. I messed it up bad."

"So fix it, son." His father got up. He took the few steps to the edge of the bed and clapped Hayes on the shoulder. "Fix it. And stay."

Chapter Twelve

That night, it was almost nine and nearly dark when Chrissy finally got back to her parents' house. Her workday at the inn had been endless, just one mini-disaster after another.

But somehow, she'd lived through it. Now she needed a long bath and maybe a good book to get lost in, something to keep her mind off Hayes and everything they could have had if only—

Her thoughts flew off in all directions. Because right there, in front of her mother's house, sat Hayes's big, black crew cab.

"What the…?" she whispered to no one in particular, slamming on the brakes a split second before she plowed right into the back of the dusty black truck that should not even be there.

But it was.

About then, she dared to turn her head and glance toward the house.

After blinking twice to make certain she wasn't seeing things, she finally believed that Hayes Parker was sitting in one of the Adirondack chairs on her parents' front porch wearing faded jeans and that black leather jacket of his, the glow from the porchlight picking up glints of gold in his brown hair. As she stared, he got up.

And she just sat there behind the wheel as he came down the front walk, her pulse pounding so hard she thought she might be having a heart attack or something. He came around to the driver's side. Her window was open, and she hadn't summoned the presence of mind to shut it before he got there.

He leaned in. "Hey."

She closed her eyes, turned her head to stare out the windshield, and opened them again. He was way too close. His scent tempted her—leather, soap and man.

She couldn't make herself turn and look at him. Instead, she scowled at the dusty back end of his big pickup. "What's up?"

"Your mom said I could wait on the porch. She said you'd be home before seven. I was beginning to worry."

She glared hard straight ahead. "What do you want, Hayes?"

He didn't answer for the longest time. She was about to roll up the window, back up, drive around his truck and keep going until she was somewhere he wasn't when he finally spoke in a rough whisper. "Come for a ride with me, Chrissy."

No, Hayes. Never. Those words were right there on the tip of her tongue.

But for some unknown reason, she couldn't push them out of her mouth.

"Why?" she asked instead.

Silence. She wasn't surprised. Of course he had no answer to her simple, one-word question.

But then he said, "Because I screwed up. Again. Because if you give me one more chance, I promise that this time, I will finally get it right."

She turned her head toward him slowly. His eyes said it all. He was telling the truth.

* * *

"Where are we going?" she asked five minutes later. She was sitting in the passenger seat of his crew cab by then.

He had the wheel. "A certain spot on the ranch, under a cottonwood on the banks of a creek."

She remembered. "Our first time…"

"That's right. And our second time, too."

They left the lights of town in the rearview. Soon, they were bumping along a dirt road on Parker land, the quarter moon leading them on. She spotted that cottonwood ahead and to the right. He kept going, finally turning the wheel, leaving the dusty road behind to bump along up a rise of land and stop under the branches of that old tree.

From where they sat, the land sloped down toward the creek below. The water shimmered in the light of the waning moon.

Reaching over the seat, he grabbed a blanket and tucked it under his arm. Then he shoved open his door, got out and came around to her side.

When he pulled open her door and held out his hand, she took it. He helped her down. Together, they spread the blanket under the tree.

"Take your shoes off. Have a seat," he said.

Out of nowhere, she felt awkward, in her work skirt, cotton shirt and short vest. But she did as he suggested, slipping off her practical pumps, setting them out of the way before dipping to sit and folding her legs to the side.

When he dropped down next to her, she tugged on her skirt to keep it from riding up her thighs. *Breathe*, she thought. *Just breathe and everything will be all right.* "Okay, Hayes. I'm listening."

He leaned in and whispered so tenderly, "I love you, Chrissy Hastings. I love you with all my heart." Her breath caught when he said those perfect words. And he wasn't finished. "One more chance," he said. "That's all I'm asking."

Yes! her heart cried. But she couldn't quite give him that. Not yet. She muttered, "Well, you're asking a lot."

"I know it. And I can't say I'd blame you if you turned me down flat. But still, I am asking for just one more chance, Chrissy. Please."

She met his eyes. Emotion rose inside her, making her throat clutch. "You hurt me. You really hurt me. Fifteen years ago. And last Saturday night, too."

He slowly nodded. "I know. I just hope you can forgive me. I had it in my head that I was done with love. But that was just fear talking. Looking back, I think I knew from that first day, when I walked into the inn and there you were, more beautiful even than I remembered, saying my name, reminding me of everything we had together, of all we lost because I was too proud, too scared and too messed up to wait for you when you asked me to. That first day at the inn, I thought I was smarter than I used to be, that I'd learned from my losses, that I wouldn't be screwing up in the same old ways all over again."

"But you did."

"Yes, I did. Can you forgive me?"

Really, there was only one answer to that question. She gave it. "Of course."

He blinked at her, stunned.

She took his hand and kept her eyes locked with his. "I forgive you, Hayes. Because I love you, too."

"Damn," he whispered prayerfully. "I didn't appreciate those words as much as I should have when you said them last Saturday night. Would you say them once more?"

"I love you, Hayes. I truly do."

He pulled her close. It was the sweetest moment. It meant

the world to her, just having his arms around her again. They shared a long, sweet kiss.

When he lifted his head, he said, "I'm staying here in Tenacity, Chrissy. My dad and I, we had a big blow up, but then we finally sat down and had a long talk. He wants me to stay and run the ranch. I'm going to do it."

She pressed her hand to the side of his face. "I'm so glad."

"We've got a lot of work ahead of us, my dad and me, but I believe we'll make it through."

"I *know* you will."

His eyes were shining. "Would you consider moving back into the ranch house, but this time on a permanent basis?"

"What are you asking me, Hayes?"

"I want you with me. I'm trying not to rush you, but now that I finally see what I want most of all, showing restraint on this subject is pretty damn difficult."

"You want me to live at the ranch with you?"

"I want you however I can get you. If you need to move back to your condo, we'll work it out. But what I really want is for you to share the room at the end of the upstairs hall with me for real. And not just for a few hours at night in secret. I want us together. I want that so much. Will you marry me, Chrissy?"

She gasped. And then her throat clutched up again. Her eyes blurred with tears.

"Hey," he whispered. "Hey…" And he took her face so gently between his two rough hands. "Am I pushing too fast?"

She shook her head. "No."

"Well, then, is this about kids? Are you worried because you can't have them? Because I swear to you, I really don't care if you can have my babies or not. Yeah, I want a family. But I'm more than willing to adopt or try some sort of artificial insemination…or not." He brushed a tear from her cheek with his thumb. Now he looked really worried. "I mean it, Chrissy. However it works out, kids or no kids, as long as it's you and me together, we can make it through."

That did it, a sob escaped her. And then she burst into tears.

"Aw, my darlin'." Again, he wrapped her in those strong arms and pressed a kiss into her hair. "It's okay. I promise you. It will be all right."

Sagging against him, she slowly got the tears under control. Swiping the moisture off her cheeks, she pulled away enough to meet his eyes. "Oh, Hayes. I wasn't hesitating, I promise you. I'm just so happy right now, and that made me cry."

He still looked way too concerned.

So she took his hand, pressed it to her heart and said, "It's like this, about the fertility thing. I'm always vague when I talk about what went wrong between Sam and me. People usually assume I must have been the one with the issue. And I let them assume that. My ex-husband is a proud man, and no way am I putting his secrets on the street. But after three years of trying to get pregnant the usual way, Sam and I finally went to a specialist. First thing, we were both tested. We found out then that Sam was sterile. And he couldn't handle that. He just didn't know how to deal with the fact that he would never physically father a child."

"So, you're saying…"

"I'm saying that all my tests indicated I'm perfectly capable of having a baby whenever we decide to get going on that."

"Wow." He nodded slowly. "Well, then. All right. So there's no problem, huh?"

"Oh, Hayes. There are always problems. Problems are part of life."

"But you're willing to face all those problems anyway, with me?"

"Yes," she whispered, and then she flung her arms around his neck and pulled him down onto the blanket.

They celebrated their reunion right then and there, at the spot where they'd first made love all those years and years ago. It was perfect, just the two of them, naked under that tree with the quarter moon watching over them from way up high in the night sky.

That Friday in the early afternoon, they drove to Bronco for a weekend getaway, just the two of them. They stayed at a nice hotel in Bronco Heights.

Saturday morning, after breakfast in bed, Hayes got down on one knee and held up a beautiful vintage diamond ring, a classic solitaire on a gold band. "Chrissy Hastings, you made me the happiest man in Montana when you said you would marry me. But there's a little something I left out of my proposal and it's time I made that right. Would you do me the honor of accepting this—"

Before he could finish that sentence, Chrissy leapt from the bed, sat on his bended knee and threw her arms around him. "Oh, Hayes… Yes! Absolutely. Yes." She peppered kisses all over his face.

He laughed. "You're sure about this now?"

"So sure. And never surer about anything in my whole life, ever, I promise you."

He kissed her lips, lightly. Tenderly. "This ring was my Grandma Tessa's. My mom gave it to me yesterday. But if you'd rather have something new, something that you get to choose—"

She clapped her hand over his mouth. "I love it. It's perfect. Nothing could possibly suit me better."

"Well, all right then." He slipped his grandmother's ring on her finger.

She held out her hand and admired the sparkling stone. "It's so beautiful. Oh, Hayes. I don't think I've ever been this happy."

He scooped her up against his chest and stood. "Let's celebrate."

And they did, right there in the wide, comfy bed.

Later, they walked up and down the streets near their hotel, holding hands, pausing to admire the displays in the shop windows. They'd wandered for a while when Chrissy spotted the big stone building on the corner.

She tugged on his hand. "Hayes…"

"What?"

"I have an idea."

"What kind of idea?"

"You'll see. Come with me." She led him to the end of the street and pointed at the three-story building across a thick, green stretch of lawn. "City Hall."

He seemed puzzled. "Should I be impressed?"

"No, Hayes." She took him by the shoulders, went on tiptoe and whispered in his ear, "You should marry me. Today."

He blinked down at her. "Are you serious?"

"Oh, yes, I am."

"But I thought you would want a big church wedding."

She shook her head. "What I want is forever with you starting right now. I want our marriage to begin today…" Suddenly, her confidence wavered. She added in a softer voice, "I mean, if you want that, too…"

He pulled her closer and kissed her. "Nothing would make me happier. Marry me, Chrissy. Marry me today."

"Yes!" she shouted loud enough that a couple of tall

cowboys stopped right there on the street to stare. Chrissy didn't care. She had her arms around her man, and she kissed him again, a long kiss, slow and deep.

When he lifted his head, he said, "We have to go back to the hotel first, though."

She frowned up at him, puzzled. "We do?"

He nodded. "My Grandma Tessa's wedding band. I left it in the room safe." She grabbed his hand. "Well, come on, then. Let's get that ring and make it happen."

An hour later, they were married. She had his grand-mother's wedding band on her finger, with three sweet diamonds glittering along the band, a perfect match for the engagement ring he'd given her earlier.

"I can't believe we did it," she said. "We're married, you and me. After all these years, we're finally married…"

He nodded. "It's a good day, Chrissy Parker."

"The best," she agreed. Laughing, she grabbed his hand again and pulled him over to the town bulletin board on the wall near the double doors that led outside. "Let's see what's going on in Bronco." She studied the flyers announcing upcoming events. "Hmm. I see there are back-to-back picnics coming up in beautiful Bronco Park. And then there's the Golden Buckle Anniversary event, the Mistletoe Rodeo in November, and of course the Christmas tree lighting in December."

He pulled her close and kissed her. "We'll need to come back."

"Often," she added.

"It's a plan," he agreed.

She leaned closer to the board. "What's this? Oh, Hayes, it's a Missing Person poster about Winona Cobbs."

Hayes asked, "The famous psychic, right?"

"Yeah."

He was frowning. "It says here that she disappeared."

Chrissy nodded. "Yes, she did. She vanished on the day before her wedding to Stanley Sanchez. Stanley's younger than Winona, only in his eighties—oh, Hayes. Nobody knows where she went. We all keep hoping she'll just show up again somehow. But she hasn't. And that can't be good. It's been a month now…"

"Hey." He pulled her closer. "I'm sure they'll find her."

"Oh, I hope so."

He kissed the tip of her nose. "She's Winona Cobbs. Never count her out."

"You're right. Winona is a force of nature. I'm sure she'll be back. She and Stanley will be reunited. Just wait and see."

"Yeah. Impossible things happen all the time. I mean, look at us, Mrs. Parker. After fifteen years and a whole raft of heartbreak, here we are, together forever. At last."

"At last," she echoed, holding up her ring finger, admiring the way the diamonds sparkled in the light.

"I love you, Chrissy." He tipped up her chin with a tender hand.

"And I love you, Hayes. So much."

And then, oblivious to the citizens of Bronco bustling in and out the double doors a few feet away, they shared another slow, sweet kiss.

* * * * *

Look for the next installment in the new continuity
Montana Mavericks: The Trail to Tenacity
The Maverick Makes the Grade
by USA TODAY bestselling author Stella Bagwell.
On sale September 2024,
wherever Harlequin books and ebooks are sold.